THE
MONEY
SHOT

BOOKS BY STUART WOODS

FICTION

Turbulence[†]

Shoot First[†]

Unbound[†]

Quick & Dirty[†]

Indecent Exposure[†]

Fast & Loose[†]

Below the Belt[†]

Sex, Lies & Serious Money[†]

Dishonorable Intentions[†]

Family Jewels[†]

Scandalous Behavior[†]

Foreign Affairs[†]

Naked Greed[†]

Hot Pursuit[†]

Insatiable Appetites[†]

Paris Match[†]

Cut and Thrust[†]

Carnal Curiosity[†]

Standup Guy[†]

Doing Hard Time[†]

Unintended Consequences[†]

Collateral Damage[†]

Severe Clear[†]

Unnatural Acts[†]

D.C. Dead[†]

Son of Stone[†]

Bel-Air Dead[†]

Strategic Moves[†]

Santa Fe Edge[§]

Lucid Intervals[†]

Kisser[†]

Hothouse Orchid[*]

Loitering with Intent[†]

Mounting Fears[‡]

Hot Mahogany[†]

Santa Fe Dead[§]

Beverly Hills Dead

Shoot Him If He Runs[†]

Fresh Disasters[†]

Short Straw[§]

Dark Harbor[†]

Iron Orchid[*]

Two-Dollar Bill[†]

The Prince of Beverly Hills

Reckless Abandon[†]

Capital Crimes[‡]

Dirty Work[†]

Blood Orchid[*]

The Short Forever[†]

Orchid Blues[*]

Cold Paradise[†]

L.A. Dead[†]

The Run[‡]

Worst Fears Realized[†]

Orchid Beach[*]

Swimming to Catalina[†]

Dead in the Water[†]	New York Dead[†]
Dirt[†]	Palindrome
Choke	Grass Roots[‡]
Imperfect Strangers	White Cargo
Heat	Deep Lie[‡]
Dead Eyes	Under the Lake
L.A. Times	Run Before the Wind[‡]
Santa Fe Rules[§]	Chiefs[‡]

COAUTHORED BOOKS

The Money Shot[**]
(with Parnell Hall)

Barely Legal[††]
(with Parnell Hall)

Smooth Operator[**]
(with Parnell Hall)

TRAVEL

A Romantic's Guide to the Country Inns of Britain and Ireland (1979)

MEMOIR

Blue Water, Green Skipper

[*]A Holly Barker Novel	[§]An Ed Eagle Novel
[†]A Stone Barrington Novel	[**]A Teddy Fay Novel
[‡]A Will Lee Novel	[††]A Herbie Fisher Novel

THE MONEY SHOT

STUART WOODS

and PARNELL HALL

G. P. PUTNAM'S SONS   NEW YORK

PUTNAM

G. P. Putnam's Sons
Publishers Since 1838
An imprint of Penguin Random House LLC
375 Hudson Street
New York, New York 10014

Library of Congress Cataloging-in-Publication Data

Names: Woods, Stuart, author. | Hall, Parnell, author.
Title: The money shot / Stuart Woods, Parnell Hall.
Description: New York : G. P. Putnam's Sons, 2018. |
Series: A Teddy Fay novel ; 2
Identifiers: LCCN 2018000922 | ISBN 9780735218598 (hardcover) |
ISBN 9780735218604 (ebook)
Subjects: LCSH: Intelligence officers—United States—Fiction. |
BISAC: FICTION / Action & Adventure. | FICTION / Suspense. | FICTION /
Thrillers. | GSAFD: Suspense fiction. | Mystery fiction.
Classification: LCC PS3573.O642 M66 2018 | DDC 813/.54—dc23
LC record available at https://lccn.loc.gov/2018000922
p.   cm.

Printed in the United States of America
1   3   5   7   9   10   8   6   4   2

BOOK DESIGN BY LUCIA BERNARD

THE
MONEY
SHOT

1

Teddy Fay crouched behind the parked car and waited for the man to come out the door. He screwed the silencer onto his gun and checked the sight. He didn't have to. Teddy had designed the gun himself, a silent killing machine that didn't miss.

The door creaked open, but it was a woman who emerged, an attractive woman in an evening gown. She came down the steps and walked off down the street.

The door opened again. This time it was his quarry, the young man he'd seen in the window above. He came down the front steps, unaware of any danger.

Teddy stepped up behind him and placed the muzzle of the silenced gun against his neck.

The man froze. Young, handsome, clueless, he murmured, "Wait."

Three shots rang out.

Teddy's body jackknifed away. A river of crimson gushed from his chest. His gun, unfired, wavered and fell away from his target. He slumped to the pavement, his eyes registering shock and pain.

A young woman stepped out of the shadows. She had a gun in her hand. A myriad of emotions registered on her face, from grim resolution to blessed relief coupled with an overwhelming loss of innocence. She swayed slightly, and the young man enfolded her in his arms.

"Cut!" Peter Barrington said. After checking with camera and sound, he added, "And that's a print. Okay, let's get him cleaned up, we're going again."

The crew began resetting the scene. A gofer and a second assistant director helped Teddy to his feet.

Peter conferred with his actors. "Excellent, Tessa. I never get tired of seeing you shoot him."

"Thanks a bunch," Teddy said.

Peter turned to the young man Teddy was going to shoot. "Brad, wonderful work, but the line is 'please,' not 'wait.'"

Brad Hunter was a movie star. He could argue with a director. "I just can't see Devon saying 'please.'"

"I hear what you're saying, but we still need to see the fear. A split second. That cold, icy panic that surges through your veins as you know this is it. Your fans will still love you, they won't think you a coward. They'll think you're a great actor. Plus they'll love the character who masters his fear and is brave in the face of death. Trust me on this."

Peter always gave Teddy notes, too, so Brad wouldn't think he was picking on him. "Nice job," Peter told him, "but I can't help feeling like you're waiting to be shot."

"I am," Teddy said. "If I were doing it, I'd have stepped up and shot him in the head. He wouldn't have had time to say 'please.'"

"Yes, but you're not you. You're Leonard Kirk, a cold-blooded killer and a dangerous man, but not infallible. The type of man who might make a mistake through arrogance. He *wants* to hear his victims say please."

Teddy grinned. "You couldn't just rewrite the script and let me shoot Brad?"

"It might change the plot a little."

Peter Barrington was shooting a scene from his new film, *Desperation at Dawn*, on location on the streets of L.A. It was a night shoot, which was hard enough to light without all the special effects. If the blood from the blood bags wasn't lit just right it appeared fake, which of course it was. And the moonlight had to reflect off the cold steel of Teddy's gun. There was a huge difference between an adequate shot and a good shot. Some directors didn't know it. They worked with the actors, and that was it. Peter Barrington was on top of everything. That's why his films were so good.

The second AD led Teddy back to the makeup and wardrobe trailer. Part of the second assistant director's job was being in charge of the cast, keeping track of where the actors were at all times and seeing they made it to the set. Actors had a tendency to wander, hence they were escorted even to places they knew well. Teddy sat down at the makeup counter, where a swarm of crew members from props, special effects, makeup, hair, and wardrobe stripped off his shirt and removed the spent squibs and blood bags that provided the shooting effect.

Marsha Quickly, the actress who came out of the door before the shooting, was touching up her makeup in the chair next to his. She smiled at Teddy. "How many times do I have to watch you get shot?"

Teddy grinned. "You love it and you know it."

"Don't be silly."

"Turns you on, doesn't it?"

Teddy Fay, aka producer Billy Barnett, aka weapons expert and stuntman Mark Weldon, had evolved into a character actor as the man you loved to hate. His on-screen presence had tested so highly, Peter had begun using him regularly. Teddy had adopted the screen name Mark Weldon so as not to draw attention to the producer Billy Barnett. With Teddy's facility for makeup, there was no danger of anyone recognizing him on-screen.

A costume lady wiped the blood off Teddy's chest and helped him into a clean white shirt. She left it unbuttoned so they could hang the fresh blood bags.

"I haven't seen you on the set before," Teddy said to the actress. "Are you shooting tomorrow?"

"I wish. I'm a Day Player, just in the one scene."

Day Player was a bit of an exaggeration. Marsha was actually a Silent Bit, an extra with no lines but a specific action. In Marsha's case it involved walking out the door.

Teddy nodded sympathetically.

Iris, the makeup lady, tapped his cheek and gave him her

patented if-you-wouldn't-mind smile once she had his attention. Teddy shrugged helplessly to the actress, then sat up straight and faced the makeup mirror like a good boy while Iris touched him up.

M arsha side-spied Mark Weldon and wondered if he was worth making a play for. He was certainly handsome enough, but could he help her career? Marsha hated to be so mercenary, but it was tough in L.A. for an actress, at least for one getting nothing but two-second, silent-bit parts. She decided he probably wasn't worth pursuing. A name actor might help her, but a stuntman in the film just to get killed wouldn't have much clout.

The wig Mark had been using as a villain was askew, having slipped when he slid to the ground. As Iris adjusted it, Marsha was struck by the familiarity of the face underneath.

She knew him. In her former life as Bambi, a cocktail waitress and shill at the New Desert Inn and Casino, a high-end casino in Las Vegas, she had known him as Billy Burnett, a high roller who had run off with one of casino boss Pete Genaro's right-hand girls. The last she had heard, Genaro was moving heaven and earth to find her.

Marsha smiled. What little extra work she'd been getting lately hadn't been paying the rent. She wondered what this little tidbit of information might be worth.

2

P ete Genaro, the owner and operator of the New Desert Inn and Casino, answered the phone with his customary growl. "Genaro."

"Hey, Pete," Marsha laughed. "Don't bite my head off. I'm on your side."

"Who's this?"

"Marsha Quickly."

"Who?"

"Bambi. I used to work for you."

Genaro searched his memory for a Bambi and seemed to remember a cocktail waitress with blond hair and long legs.

"Oh, yeah. What's up? You want your job back?"

"No, I'm an actress now out in Hollywood. I'm doing fine," she lied. "Of course, one can always use some spare change. I have a tip for you. The high roller who ran off with one of your girls—Billy Burnett, wasn't it? The guy who ran off with Charmaine?"

"What about him?"

"I just ran into him on a movie set. He's changed his appearance, and he's working as a stuntman."

"Are you sure it's him?"

"I saw them touching up his makeup."

"Oh? That's interesting."

Genaro took down the information. He'd send Bambi, or whatever she was calling herself these days, a nice bonus to keep the contact open, but she was out of date with her news. Genaro had been trying to find Billy Burnett, had even hired a skip tracer to find him. Not because he cared about some high roller making off with a girl—the girls were a dime a dozen—but rather, at the insistence of one of his guests and board members, a Russian gentleman who proved so odious Genaro had him voted off the board of directors and ousted him from the hotel. He then warned Billy Burnett, whom the skip tracer had found working at Centurion Pictures under the name of Billy Barnett, that the Russian was coming. So Genaro had no intention of acting on Bambi's hot tip. He just filed the information for future reference.

At the moment, Genaro had other things on his mind. Sammy Candelosi had just purchased the casino next door. That couldn't be good. Genaro didn't know Sammy Candelosi, but the man was reputed to have mob connections, and was not to be trifled with. Genaro had no intention of trifling with him. He intended to give Sammy a wide berth.

Genaro's intercom buzzed.

"What is it?" he growled irritably.

"Sammy Candelosi is here to see you."

Genaro scowled. "Send him in."

3

Sammy Candelosi looked like he'd just stepped out of a barbershop. His curly black hair was neatly trimmed, his cheeks razor-smooth. He gave the impression he was professionally shaved every day. His dark blue suit could have financed a small casino. His black leather shoes gleamed, and his steely gray eyes never blinked, giving the impression that they missed nothing.

"I'm so glad we could have this meeting," Sammy said. Somehow he acted as if he were the host. "This is my associate, Mr. Slythe."

Slythe wore a pale blue turtleneck instead of a tie, and an off-white suit. His look was not welcoming. He neither smiled nor gestured. His eyes were calculating, constantly taking in information.

Genaro had a goon on hand for muscle. "This is my associate, Jake. Gentlemen, please be seated."

Sammy was already pulling up a chair.

Pete Genaro smoldered and tried to think of some way he could regain the upper hand.

"So, have you ever run a casino before, Mr. Candelosi?"

"I've been *in* them," Sammy said.

Genaro wasn't sure if it was a joke. "Well, they don't run themselves. You need good people. The money's steady, but it's work."

"The money's *steady?*" Sammy said.

"It is."

"Shouldn't it be *increasing?*"

"It is. A steady increase."

"Again with the word 'steady.'"

Genaro frowned. "What are you trying to say?"

Sammy lit a cigar, looking around for an ashtray. Genaro moved one across the desk for him. Sammy flicked his cigar in that general direction. "You've been in this business a long time."

"I have. I know the ins and outs, if there's anything you need to know."

"I need to know why you're not rich."

Pete Genaro's mouth fell open. "I beg your pardon?"

Sammy shrugged. "A casino is a gold mine. It mints money. People bring money to it, leave money in it, and take away nothing. There's no product. In any other business, you're selling something. Say it's olive oil: You have it, you sell it, you run low, you need to restock your supply. But with a casino, people show up and happily plunk their money down to buy nothing. Money for nothing. That's the best business in the world. So I take a look at your casino as I walk in, and I'm saying to myself, that's a pretty nice operation. They should be making more money. So I'm thinking, how can we make that happen?" Sammy took a puff on his cigar. "Seems to me the easiest thing for me to do is buy you out."

Genaro was dumbfounded. "What?"

"I mean, here we are, next door to each other, in competition with each other. How much better to pool our resources? If I were to buy you out and run both organizations at the same time, think of the cost benefit. Some of middle management would become redundant, and there would be no reason to waste money attempting to lure players away from each other."

"We don't do that."

"Oh, no? I comp a high roller a suite, you comp him a suite and a hooker. I have nothing against gamblers getting laid, but why should I pay for it?"

"Mr. Candelosi, I have no intention of selling."

"Don't you have a board of directors? Wouldn't they have to consider a bid?" Sammy flicked his ash. "Anyway, assuming a merger might be in store, any accommodation I can make, or any advice you might have on the operation of a casino, I'm not too old a dog to learn a new trick."

Sammy smiled and spread his arms, as if they were the best of friends.

S on of a bitch!" Genaro growled.

Jake, on his way back from seeing Sammy out, said, "Who?"

"Who do you think? Sammy fucking Candelosi! He knows I'm not going to sell. That wasn't a genuine offer. That was just posturing, strutting his stuff, trying to assert himself because he's the new kid in town and he doesn't like it. Well, he picked the wrong man to meddle with." Genaro jerked his thumb. "Get over there and find out what he's doing."

"How do I do that?"

"Say I sent you to help him."

"Why would you do that?"

"To find out what he's doing!"

"But—"

"Hey, you say I sent you to help. He won't buy it, but you get to look around. Talk to his goon."

"He don't look like he talks much."

"Give it a shot. The worst that happens is it doesn't work."

"The worst that happens is he shoots me in the fuckin' head."

Genaro shrugged. "Then we'll know it didn't work."

Pete Genaro didn't know who he was dealing with. Sammy Candelosi sized Jake up as the Trojan horse he knew him to be, and asked Jake to walk the floor with his man Slythe to tell him who his best men were. Jake, who had no idea which employees were any good, pointed out a dealer and pit boss just because he knew their names.

The next morning, the pit boss was found floating facedown in his swimming pool, and the dealer's car blew up.

The police had no problem following the trail from Sammy and Slythe, who volunteered that Genaro's man Jake had identified the victims as Sammy's best men, to Jake, who admitted he'd done that, to Pete Genaro, who was apoplectic. He was certainly the most likely suspect in the two murders, but he was innocent. Sammy Candelosi had killed his own men just to get him in trouble.

But try to make the cops believe that.

The cops didn't have enough evidence to arrest Genaro, but by the time they were gone, one thing was clear.

Pete Genaro had backed into the middle of an undeclared mob war.

4

eddy Fay watched from the sidelines as Tessa Tweed Bacchetti and Brad Hunter finished up their scene on the soundstage on the Centurion Pictures back lot. Brad was the name above the title, and Tessa a featured actress, but for Teddy's money, she was playing him off the stage.

Peter and Ben had discovered Tessa when they first started at Centurion Pictures. A young British actress, Tessa had been in town to visit her mother, who was staying with Peter's father, Stone Barrington, at the time. The boys wangled Tessa a screen test. She photographed well, and read even better, and wound up winning a part.

She also won the heart of Ben Bacchetti, Peter's best friend and the future head of Centurion Studios. She'd been working steadily ever since, and not just because of her husband's position. She really was that good.

Teddy enjoyed watching her. Teddy enjoyed most everything about the movies. He liked producing them in his persona of Billy Barnett, and he got a real kick out of playing the villain in his new guise of Mark Weldon. Teddy could shoot people with no repercussions whatsoever. People liked him to do it, as long as he didn't bump off the hero. As long as he got his retribution in the end.

Teddy understood the premise, but he didn't entirely buy it. He could envision a script where he wound up killing the hero and getting away. He wondered if he could sell Peter on the idea.

On the movie set, Tessa delivered her last line.

"Cut," Peter said. "And that's a new setup. It's a camera move. Actors, take a break until called, but don't go far. Our crew is good."

Tessa sought Teddy out as soon as she was off the set. "Was I all right?"

"You were great."

"I felt a little off."

"With you, a little off is sensational."

"Don't kid me. I'm serious."

"So am I. You're acting rings around the guy. If you ask me, they've got the credits flip-flopped."

Tessa wasn't up to playful banter. "Listen. Can I talk to you?"

Teddy saw the anxiety in her eyes, but gave no sign. He simply said, "Let's get a cup of coffee."

Teddy took Tessa down to the commissary. Actors and crew members filled most of the tables.

"It's crowded," Tessa said.

"Sure," Teddy said. "Everyone can hear us, so no one will bother to listen to us. Come on."

They got cups of coffee and found an unoccupied table near the back.

Teddy took a gulp of coffee and smiled a huge smile for the benefit of anyone who might be looking their way. "Okay," he said, "what's wrong?"

Tessa took a breath. "I'm being blackmailed."

"What?" Teddy said incredulously.

"At least I think I am."

"You *think* you are?"

"I received a letter."

"With a blackmail demand?"

"No."

Teddy blinked.

Tessa put up her hands. "I know, I know, I'm telling it badly. I'm upset."

"What was in the letter?"

"A photo."

Teddy nodded. "I see. A photo of what?"

Tessa stirred her coffee as if she couldn't quite meet his eyes. "I had a boyfriend at university."

"I'm shocked. What university?"

"Oxford."

"Go on. Who was the boyfriend?"

"Nigel Hightower the Third. He looks just like he sounds, the type of boy who'd fit right in at Ascot or the local racquet club."

"A real Prince Charming."

"On the surface."

"Oh?"

"You know how you think you know someone and they turn out to be someone else?"

Teddy smiled. In his twenty years at the CIA, not to mention the years since leaving it, he had found that to be true more often than not. Teddy's default mode was suspicious.

"Go on," he said.

"Well, that's how it was with Nigel. When I was with him, it all seemed so ideal. We were in college, we had no concerns, nothing more to deal with than classes. Only we weren't in the same fields. I was studying acting, and he was getting a gentleman's C. Anyway, it was idyllic, and he was so romantic. It never occurred to me he would do such a thing."

"And what did he do?"

"He filmed me without my knowledge."

"In bed?"

"Yes."

"With him?"

She nodded.

"And showed it to people?"

"I don't think he did. I think he just hung on to it."

"You never knew about it?"

"I found out. It was one of the reasons we broke up."

"You didn't take the tape?"

"He said he destroyed it. I thought he was telling the truth—he was never malicious, just used poor judgment. I should have known better."

"If he held on to the tape and never showed anyone, what happened?"

"I became famous, or at least I have a career in pictures. I think he couldn't help bragging he'd once dated a movie star."

"Oh?"

"I'm assuming he shot his mouth off, got drunk and bragged about the tape."

"And that's what the photo is?"

"It was a still from the video. At least that's what the letter said. They said it was just a sample, they had the whole thing, and if I didn't want anyone to see the tape, I'd do exactly as they say."

"Which is?"

"They didn't tell me yet. I'm to await further instructions."

"What about the letter?"

"It came through the mail. It was typed. No return address."

"Do you think it's your ex-boyfriend who's doing this?"

"Nigel? No, he wouldn't. That's not his style. He'd do something dumb, sure. Something weak and cowardly, like brag to impress someone. But blackmail? I don't see it."

"No one's asked you for money," Teddy pointed out.

Tessa frowned. "You mean, could this just be his way of coming back into my life?"

"It's a thought. Is it possible?"

"It seems farfetched. I'm married, after all."

Teddy smiled. "That's often not a deal breaker."

"I'm not ruling it out. I just don't think it is."

"Let me ask you this. Did you keep a copy of the tape?"

"No."

"I'm thinking maybe he gave you the tape, saying it was the original, and you found out later he kept a copy."

"No, I told you. He said he destroyed it."

"And he never gave you a copy?"

"No. If there was a copy, I never knew it."

Teddy frowned.

"What's the big idea?" Tessa said.

"I'm just trying to figure out how someone could have gotten his hands on it if it *wasn't* through Nigel."

Tessa shook her head. "There's no way. I swear, I never had a tape."

Teddy frowned again.

Tessa looked at him with pleading eyes. "So, what can I do?"

Teddy considered. "Where's the letter?"

"In my purse."

"Let me have it."

"You're going to look at the photo?"

"I don't need the photo. Just the letter."

Tessa opened her purse and pulled out the letter. It was in a standard white business-sized envelope. She opened it, took out the photo, and put it back in her purse. She started to take the letter out of the envelope.

"No, the whole thing," Teddy said. He slipped the letter into his jacket pocket. "Okay, it's in my hands now. You've got a movie to make. Concentrate on that."

"What are you going to do?"

"Let me worry about that. For the moment, no one's asked you for anything. The minute they do, you come to me."

5

Mason Kimble pressed Play again. He never got tired of watching the video. Ben Bacchetti's wife. It was almost too good to be true.

Ben Bacchetti had shot down his project. A Kimble & Cardigan picture was not good enough for Centurion, not "classy" enough. Bacchetti had treated him like a B-movie producer, and he would pay for the insult.

The only thing you needed to make a film classy was a studio logo. Slap "Centurion Studios Presents" on the front of any one of his films, and suddenly it would be respectable, getting the better bookings, going into the better theaters. With studio backing, his profits would soar.

Mason snatched up the remote control and rewound the video to the scene he liked. Mason had to hook up a DVD player so he could watch it in his office, instead of stepping into the editing room, but it was worth it. He liked to watch it from *his* desk, with the posters on the wall behind him from *his* pictures, *Girl on the Edge, Sheila's Last Chance*. So what if his "studio" was a second-floor walk-up over a lingerie shop? His pictures made money.

Granted, Centurion's pictures made money, too, with the exception of the occasional highbrow film made for limited release in artsy little theaters, some of which didn't even sell popcorn, for Christ's sake. They might break even, but what was the point? All of Mason's pictures made money, just not as much as they'd make with the Centurion logo and the wider distribution that came with it.

But Ben Bacchetti, the arrogant prick, had shot him down, and Mason Kimble was back to square one.

Then Mason's father, the eccentric tobacco mogul, died intestate—at least, no one could find his will—and suddenly Mason had the wherewithal to make a B-movie studio legit.

And pay Ben Bacchetti back in the process.

Mason froze the video on his favorite shot. It was much more revealing than the one he had sent to Tessa Bacchetti.

"And there's the money shot," he murmured.

Mason enjoyed it for a while, then ejected the DVD and locked it in his wall safe.

6

Teddy went back to the house he maintained as producer Billy Barnett. It still gave him a pang, even after all this time, to be in the home where he and Charmaine had lived as man and wife. When he'd stolen her away from Pete Genaro, she'd married him and taken the name Elizabeth Barnett. As Betsy Barnett, she'd worked as Peter's assistant at Centurion Studios. Then her life had been cruelly snuffed out by a drunken driver. Teddy had made sure those responsible had paid, and had moved on with a short relationship with a woman he met during the process. But Sally's home was in New Mexico and his was here, and in the end, never the twain could meet.

Teddy went into the study and fired up the computer. He scanned Tessa's blackmail letter, as well as the envelope, and ran it through a program of his own devising. It quickly identified the typeface as Helvetica, and went on to identify the brand of computer using that type, based on irregularities in the typeface itself. After careful analysis, and a few refinements of the search process, he was able to identify the particular model.

Teddy pierced a few firewalls, went straight to the manufacturer, and monitored the sales in L.A. The letter had an L.A. postmark, and the odds were it hadn't been typed elsewhere and brought to town to mail. Among the sales of that particular model of computer were a large number sold to a chain of L.A. copy shops about seven years back. Several of them had subsequently closed—not surprising with fewer and fewer people wanting hard copies in a digital age—but three were still open. A blackmailer would appreciate the anonymity offered by a copy shop computer—it might be a long shot, but Teddy never left any stone unturned. He grabbed his car keys and headed out.

The computer at the closest shop was out of order, and the computer at the second shop was working, but had an HP printer. Tessa's letter had been inked by the printer that came with the machine, not an HP. The third shop was the charm.

Teddy got on the computer and ran a search for the document, though it seemed too much to hope that the blackmailer had been idiotic enough to save it to a public machine. It was. The letter was not there. He could still have found it if it had been saved and then deleted, a pain in the ass but doable, but that wasn't the case. The letter had been typed, printed from the draft, and never saved. And that was assuming this was the right computer, no sure bet.

The chance of tracing the letter, a long shot at best, was rapidly becoming a pipe dream.

Teddy frowned, leaned back in his chair, and considered his options. He whipped out his cell phone and made a call.

7

Kevin Cushman, screen name Warplord924, was building a city in space. Much of it he was stealing from his neighbor on a nearby planet, but then Kevin had invested more of his resources in armies than construction. Conquest was the natural order of things. Warplord paid the iron price for his acquisitions.

Kevin was dressed as usual in pajamas and jockey shorts. His bed was unmade, his clothes were on the floor, and his wastebasket was crammed with the remnants of several takeout orders. A careful observer would peg him for a college dropout, rather than a highly respected computer technician grossing in the high six figures. Kevin was so good at his job that he could do it from home, and generally did. Kevin still lived with his mother, not through necessity but through inertia. Moving would have required effort.

Kevin's cell phone rang. He scooped it up to send the call to voice mail, but his eyes widened when he saw the number. He clicked it on.

"Hello?"

"Do you know who this is?"

"Yes."

"Good, then we don't have to say. I have a job for you."

"Really?"

Teddy felt a pang of guilt. The excitement in the kid's voice was palpable. Warplord had helped Teddy out during a sensitive mission, and had even been given White House access. "It's not a mission. Just a simple job."

"Oh."

"I'm sitting at a computer in a copy shop."

"That's what you need help with?"

"Yeah."

"You want me to come over?"

"I'm in Los Angeles."

"Oh. Probably not." Warplord was in D.C.

"I think someone may have typed a letter on this computer in the last few days, printed it out, but never saved it. Do you have any way of determining if that's the case?"

"What's the address of the shop?"

Teddy gave it to him, though he suspected Kevin could have tracked it on his own using Teddy's cell signal. The kid was that good.

"I assume you have a hard copy of the letter?"

"Yes. You want me to read it to you?"

"Absolutely. I'll need a key phrase."

Teddy read him the letter.

"How's that?"

"Perfect. We're in luck. The copy shop uses a basic keyword

stroke tracker, probably to flag criminal behavior, and I can use that for a search. This is not a very active terminal, which is good for us. And, bingo! The letter in question was typed on that very machine."

"I don't suppose you could tell me the name, age, and Social Security number of the guy who typed it?"

"You don't want his shoe size? I can tell you the letter was typed and printed at two-thirty yesterday afternoon. Hang on, you're in L.A. I'm always getting tripped up by time zones. Right. It's two-thirty Eastern. So it's eleven-thirty Pacific yesterday morning. The guy didn't copy the letter digitally, there was no drive hooked up to the computer at the time. Do you need anything else?"

"That's all for the time being."

"Do I get CIA clearance?"

"You did, but the job's over."

"Spoilsport," Warplord said, and went back to building space castles.

The kid at the counter was reading a movie magazine. He had longish hair, and looked like he was just waiting for some producer to walk in and make him a star.

Teddy pointed to the surveillance camera over the door. "Is that camera working?"

The kid looked up from his magazine. "You the fire inspector?"

"You think the fire inspector would be interested in the surveillance video?"

"So what's it to you?"

Teddy took out his CIA credentials and flipped them open on the counter. "There're reports of sleeper cells in the area. You know what sleeper cells are?"

"Terrorists?"

"That's right, domestic terrorists, who look just like ordinary citizens, like you and me. We think one of them came in here and used that computer in the last few days, and we need to check. So let's take a look at that camera."

The camera was working, and programmed to save the last forty-eight hours before recording over. It also had a time stamp, so Teddy was able to speed through and see who was in the shop at exactly eleven-thirty when the blackmail letter was typed.

Inexplicably, the camera was angled so as to catch the customers in the shop from the shoulders down. All Teddy could tell was the man who typed the letter was slender and wore a bespoke suit with silver-studded cuff links.

Teddy frowned.

Despite what Tessa might think, that certainly sounded like Nigel Hightower.

8

Teddy went home and ran a search for Nigel Hightower III. Nigel had dropped out of Oxford his junior year after getting involved in some sort of scandal that his father, Nigel Hightower Jr., managed to hush up. He had run afoul of the law, but the records were sealed. It took Teddy half an hour to unseal them. He would have been faster, but hacking British agencies and parsing the differences in their legal system slowed him down.

Nigel had been caught with an underage girl and two grams of cocaine. What Daddy had to pay to get him out of that one, Teddy could only imagine.

Teddy followed Nigel's trail to New York, where the young man maintained a permanent address for thirteen months, probably until Daddy cut him off. He had no reported income during that time.

Teddy next found a plane ticket to Vegas, charged against a credit card that was subsequently invalidated. Another credit card got him a hotel room at the MGM Grand, before it was revoked for lack of payment a month later.

No further credit cards were issued to Nigel Hightower, so he'd changed his name, won big, or gotten killed.

Teddy ran a global search on his name and began the tedious task of sifting through worthless responses. It was about an hour before he found a Facebook post by an Eliot Clark: "You'll never guess who I saw on the streets of L.A. Nigel Hightower. I was on a tour bus and he was walking along, but I'm sure it was him. Small world."

The post was only two weeks old.

Nigel was in L.A.

9

Teddy had dinner with the young Barringtons and Bacchettis. Teddy was quite fond of them all, and had been ever since he met Peter and Ben and Hattie driving to L.A. He'd been working at an Esso station in Mesa Grande, New Mexico, when they stopped with a flat tire. In changing it, Teddy located a tracking device placed by Russian mobsters who were intent on seeking revenge against Stone Barrington. Not wanting to alarm the young people, he'd discreetly handled the situation for them. Later he'd been pleased to catch up with them in L.A. He'd gotten a job at Centurion, first repairing prop rifles, and rapidly worked his way up to producer. Later he'd met Tessa, and watched her growing relationship with Ben. He attended the two couples' double wedding in England, and had a hand in keeping it safe.

The kids knew some, if not all, of what Teddy had done on their behalf, and they were happy to have him around in whatever identity he wished to assume.

Dinner was on the veranda of Peter and Hattie's, a huge chunk of real estate carved out of what was once the property of the Arrington Hotel. It was casual, with no cook or house-keeper involved, just burgers on the outdoor grill. Peter was flipping, and Ben was shucking corn. The girls were sunbathing by the pool and taking it easy.

Teddy gave Ben a hand with the corn.

"You look concerned," Teddy said. Ben hadn't, but it was always a good opening. You played out your line and learned what information you could unearth. In this case, Teddy wondered if Ben had noticed any tension in Tessa.

Turned out, Ben had something else on his mind.

Ben grimaced. "Not really. I don't like to bring my job home."

"I'm not home," Teddy said. "It's not like you're worrying your wife. You can tell me."

"It's no big deal. Someone's buying up Centurion stock."

"Aren't they always?"

"Sure. But this is more systematic—several long-term share-holders have sold their holdings, all within the past month."

"And that's unusual?"

"To divest themselves entirely? I'll say it is. Centurion's doing well. Even without Peter's pictures we're turning a profit, and his projects are the icing on the cake. The man makes pictures people want to see."

"So who's buying the stock?"

"It's a few holding companies, which isn't a red flag in itself. With the stock trending up, there's a chance to grab quick profits. It's just a lot of activity all at once."

"Could someone be attempting a hostile takeover?"

Ben shook his head. "It couldn't be done. We control over fifty percent of the stock."

"Are you sure?"

"Absolutely. It was tried once, when Peter's mother was alive. His father put in safeguards so it couldn't happen again. Stone has twenty-five percent. Peter and I each have fifteen. We're totally protected. I can't sell my shares without giving them the right of first refusal."

"That's right in the contract?"

"Sure. Same with the women."

"The women?"

"Marriage was an added wrinkle. What if we got divorced and the stock got split in the property settlement? Not going to happen, but you know lawyers."

Teddy put a hand on Ben's arm before he could start another husk. "Wait a minute. You're out of my area of expertise. You say you and Peter drew up contracts regarding the stocks when you got married?"

"Yes, as a precautionary measure. You know lawyers, belt and suspender types, planning for things that aren't going to happen. In the event of divorce, Hattie or Tessa must sell the stock back to us at par value."

"Did Stone draw up the contract himself?"

"No, he was afraid of conflict of interest. He had Herbie Fisher do it. He's one of Woodman & Weld's top lawyers. Stone swears it's ironclad."

Tessa came over and draped herself around Ben's shoulders. "What are you talking about?"

Ben grinned. "You got me. I was talking business, like a bad boy."

Tessa smiled. "I could tell when you stopped shucking corn.

Really, you men are helpless. Can't walk and chew gum at the same time." She slipped her arm through Teddy's. "Come on, Billy, leave the man alone. I'm getting hungry."

Tessa led Teddy off toward the swimming pool. When they were out of earshot, she said, "What were you really talking about?"

"We were talking about work. And if you're going to act paranoid, you might as well tell Ben the truth. Don't you think he's going to notice?" Teddy stopped by the pool. "Listen, I have to ask you something. I'm going to show you a picture, but try to look as if we're just conversing casually."

Teddy slipped his right hand in his pants pocket and slipped the photo into his hand. He pulled it out and flashed it toward Tessa, obscured from the others by his body. "Do you recognize this man?"

Tessa blinked, looked at him in exasperation. "He doesn't have a head."

"That is a drawback."

"Is this a joke?"

"No. Assuming this is the only picture we have of him, could this be anyone you know?"

"Nigel?"

"Could it be Nigel?" Teddy said.

"That's what you're thinking, isn't it? That it could be Nigel?"

"Let me put it this way. Is there anything about it that tells you it *isn't* Nigel?"

Tessa looked again.

"Those aren't his cuff links."

10

Mason Kimble and Gerard Cardigan clinked brandy snifters.

"There's nothing like a good action movie," Mason said.

"I'll say," Gerard said.

They were watching Tessa Bacchetti's sex tape. They never got tired of watching it. Mason had frozen it on the money shot in order to fill the brandy snifters. He took a sip and leaned back in his chair.

"You can sort of tell she doesn't know," Gerard said.

"Oh? How?"

"It's subtle, but it's there."

"In other words, you don't know."

"I don't know, and neither does she. That's the whole thing."

"What's the whole thing?"

"You can tell *he* knows," Gerard said. "That's how you can tell she *doesn't*. He's self-conscious and looks toward the camera, and she's uninhibited and never gives it a glance. The contrast, you see?"

Mason laughed. "Are you really finding subtext in a home sex tape?"

"No, but if we had to release this—"

"We're not."

"No, we're not," Gerard agreed. "But if we have to show it to her husband . . ." He smiled and shrugged.

"We're not doing that either."

"Worst-case scenario. We don't want *him* to think she didn't know she was being filmed. We can edit it to make sure that doesn't happen."

"How so?"

"Take out the part that makes it look like Nigel knew he was filming."

Mason saluted him with his snifter. "Good point."

Mason and Gerard were very much alike. With short haircuts, button-down collars, and bespoke suits, they looked like a couple of Ivy League frat boys, which they actually were at Princeton, before their mutual love for hazing fraternity pledges got a little out of hand. One freshman had three broken fingers. Another nearly suffocated in a junked refrigerator. They barely escaped expulsion. Mason sublimated his urges into film, Gerard into bisecting lab animals.

The boys still tended to dress alike. The only real difference was while Mason's white shirts had button cuffs, Gerard's had silver-studded cuff links.

"How's it coming with the stockholders?" Mason asked.

"The old lady's going to sell. At least I think she will. She's afraid I'm going to kill her cat."

"How did she get that impression?"

Gerard's smile was angelic. "I have no idea."

"So they're all falling into place."

"We have a problem with Miss Morgan."

"Oh?"

"She's a retired actress and sees the stock as her last connection to the movie business."

"What will it take to change her mind?"

"Nothing, I'm afraid. Her son's another story. He's a cokehead and needs the money. He'd sell it in a heartbeat."

"Too bad he doesn't own the stock."

Gerard leaned back in his chair, cocked his head, and smiled. "Isn't it?"

11

Teddy changed into his Billy Barnett attire and dropped in on the Centurion Studios accountant. Kenny was, as usual, sitting at his desk with his nose buried deep in a ledger. Teddy waited for him to emerge. He didn't.

"Hi, Kenny. How's it going?"

He looked up then, startled. "Billy. I thought you were on vacation." In order for Teddy to act in Peter's new film as stuntman Mark Weldon, Billy Barnett had officially taken a long vacation.

"I am. Just thought I'd check in."

"Oh?"

"I hear someone's buying up Centurion stock. I can't help wondering if it affects me."

Kenny was surprised. "I wouldn't think so. Aside from Stone and Ben and Peter, it hardly matters who the stockholders are."

"But it *is* being bought."

"In small amounts."

"Who's doing the buying?"

"Holding companies, largely. You don't see individuals much anymore."

"How largely?"

"You want me to add it up?"

"Please."

"Well, let's see. USB Corporation has nine percent, Venn Holding has eleven percent, Everest Holding has seven percent."

"Who are they buying it for?"

"I can't tell."

"Okay, who are they buying it *from?*"

Kenny looked. "The last transfer on the books was yesterday. Ten thousand shares. That's approximately one half of one percent."

"Who sold them?"

"Ruth Goldstone."

"Who is that?"

Kenny frowned. "Well, that is slightly odd. Ruth Goldstone is a little old lady. She's retired, lives alone with her cats. Her husband owned the stock. He died and left it to her. She likes to call me up to see how it's doing, but I guess she won't be doing that anymore."

"Does she need the money?"

"That's hardly my business," Kenny said, though he knew, and was happy to tell. "But her inheritance was not skimpy. She could afford to buy more stock, not sell it. Though she'd never make an investment of that type without her husband's guidance."

"Or a sale?"

"I was surprised," Kenny admitted.

"Then let me ask you this, and consider it comes from a paranoid producer who doesn't know what he's talking about. Could someone be attempting a hostile takeover of Centurion Pictures?"

Kenny shook his head. "Couldn't happen."

"Because the family has a controlling interest?"

"That's one reason," Kenny said. "But even if they didn't, it couldn't happen because there are some stockholders who simply would not sell."

"For instance?"

"Vanessa Morgan, for one. She has a sizable chunk." Kenny grinned. "That is a professional accounting number. 'Sizable chunk.' She wouldn't sell under any circumstances. She was a classic movie star, you probably saw her in something. She was versatile—femme fatale, ingénue, comic relief, she'd play them all. She retired when she got older though, wanted people to remember her when she was young and beautiful. Since then she's been basically a recluse. The public only gets to see her when they give her some award or other. She shows up for awards."

"She's the only one who might hold out?"

"What? Oh, the stock. No, there're others. She's the biggest and the best example. Anyway, rest assured, Vanessa Morgan isn't going to sell."

12

Gerard Cardigan dressed entirely in black. He wore tights and a leotard, as if he were a dancer, and surgical gloves, as if he were a doctor, and a black knit cap, as if he were a skier. He glided through the shadows on soft feet, barely touching the sidewalk, barely making a sound.

There was no one out at two in the morning, despite the neighborhood watch and the hired guard. The guard had a ten-block area to patrol, which was a lot of houses and a lot of streets, even if half of them were Hollywood houses with impossibly large lots. There was no way he could make a circuit in under half an hour, twenty-five minutes if he never broke stride. And a sixty-seven-year-old security guard with a fondness for tobacco was apt to break stride.

Gerard watched him go down the street and followed him from a distance, keeping him in sight until he came to the front of the house that was his target.

His path to the house was circuitous, avoiding the surveillance cameras he knew were there. He reached the vulnerable side window, the one that was wired to the security system and could be jiggled without actually disengaging the lock. He jiggled it, and faded silently into the darkness as the ear-splitting alarm woke the neighborhood.

B y the third time Vanessa Morgan's security alarm went off, the police had had it. They disconnected the damn thing and told Vanessa to call the service man in the morning, and they'd assign a car to her house for the night. Vanessa doubted that, but she was getting fed up with springing out of bed every half hour, and she wasn't keen on meeting cops in her disheveled state. She reluctantly let them turn the system off and went back to bed.

The security guard, who'd run several blocks each time the alarm went off, was having trouble catching his breath. He parked himself on the front stoop, a valiant soldier defending the unarmed castle.

While the guard manned the front door, Gerard snuck up on the house from the back. He was cautious, not being sure if the surveillance cameras were on the same circuit and had been shut off with the alarm. He reached the back terrace. An ornate metal-and-glass double door, probably dating back to the age of silent films, was easy to manipulate. Gerard opened the door a crack and slipped in.

There were no security cameras inside. Gerard knew that for a fact. Vanessa Morgan would not allow herself to appear on video short of having done her full hair and makeup, even temporarily. The thought of such footage existing at the time of her death was more than she could bear. Cameras were to keep intruders out. The perimeter was all they needed to guard.

Gerard worked his way into the center of the house, a palatial room in period style. A curved oaken staircase might have served to film *Gone with the Wind.*

Gerard crept down the hall to the master bedroom. He eased the door open and waited, listening, in case the actress was still awake.

He needn't have worried. Her adventures in the nighttime had worn her out. She was asleep by the time her head hit the pillow. Gerard stole quietly up to the bed, bent down, and clapped his hand over her mouth.

Vanessa awoke with a start. She blinked in fear and astonishment at the young man smiling down at her.

"Hello, Miss Morgan," he said. "Are you ready for your close-up?"

13

P ete Genaro's curvy secretary was flipping through the newspaper and wondering if he was going to want her to "relieve his tension," as Pete phrased it. When he'd called Sherry into his office she'd assumed that was the task at hand, but he seemed to have lost interest. That was happening a lot lately.

"Vanessa Morgan died," Sherry said. "I just saw the news headline."

Genaro looked up irritably. Everything irritated him lately. Sammy Candelosi had become a major pain in the ass, and he still hadn't figured out how to deal with him.

"Who?" Genaro said.

"Vanessa Morgan. She was a big-time classic film star. Won an Oscar."

"When?"

"A while back."

"How old was she?"

"Eighty something."

"I'm surprised she lived that long. Those stars burn themselves out."

"Not this one. She retired in her heyday, had a big contract with Centurion Pictures and just walked away."

"You remember all that?"

Sherry pointed to the paper. "Says so here. Apparently she had a big fight with the studio and wound up having to give back half her stock options. Must have cost her a fortune, but she did it."

"What was the studio?"

"Centurion Pictures. Why?"

Genaro shook his head, but the name rang a bell. He wasn't sure, but he thought that was the studio where his skip tracer had once found Billy Burnett. "When's the funeral?"

"Sunday. Were you thinking of going?" Thoughts of a trip to Hollywood danced in Sherry's head.

"I got enough shit to deal with."

Genaro went back to brooding. Funny it would be Centurion Pictures. He was pretty sure that was where they'd found Billy Burnett. And that bar girl Bambi had seen him on a movie set. Was that a Centurion picture?

Genaro wondered if Billy Burnett was still there.

14

Tyrone Flynn cleaned himself up for the funeral. He still had a runny nose and watery eyes, but that was appropriate for a man mourning the loss of his mother. Only those closest to him would have known he was celebrating his inheritance with an ounce of Peruvian flake; though the truth was Tyrone had no close friends, just fellow coke-heads and people to whom he owed money. They'd all come crawling out of the woodwork now, hoping to cash in on his bounty. He'd have to lay low for a while.

But not today. Today he had to stand in the spotlight and murmur his thanks while a seemingly endless parade of Hollywood stars offered their condolences.

It was a Hollywood funeral in every sense of the word. Vanessa Morgan might have been a recluse alive, but dead she pulled out all the stops. The cathedral she'd booked would have seated six hundred, though fewer than fifty A-list celebrities made the cut. Their selection was rumored to have been specified in her will. The lesser stars milled around outside where tents had been set up for the reception, and TV crews vied with one another for the biggest remaining names to interview.

Peter and Ben were in the church. Ben Bacchetti was invited as the head of production at Centurion Pictures. The studio had long since buried the hatchet with Vanessa, honoring her with a lifetime achievement award on the occasion of her seventy-fifth birthday. Vanessa had accepted, on the condition that her age not be advertised as the reason for the award. Peter was invited as the stepson of Vance Calder, an Academy Award–winning actor in his own right, who had acted opposite Vanessa in two of her final films. Hattie and Tessa, discreetly gorgeous in black, accompanied their husbands.

Teddy could have attended as a Centurion producer, but Billy Barnett was on vacation, and he couldn't justify showing up as stuntman Mark Weldon. Still, he had taken note of the passing of one of Centurion's largest stockholders, and, according to Kenny in Accounting, one of the least likely to sell. While the police were not treating her death as suspicious, Vanessa Morgan had not died from natural causes; she had drowned in her bathtub, and, according to the home aide who found her, her home security system had been turned off.

Gerard Cardigan watched it all from a distance. He saw Tessa Tweed Bacchetti arrive with her husband and friends and go into the church, and he saw her come out at the end of the service and climb into a limo. He was glad to see the Barringtons and Bacchettis go. He did not want to trip over them today.

Gerard mingled with the crowd until the A-list celebrities had gone and the TV crews were packing up. Then he snuck up on Tyrone Flynn, who had ducked furtively around the corner of the church. Tyrone had just unscrewed the top of a gram bottle of coke and was tapping a line out on the back of his hand. Gerard waited patiently until he snorted it and had the cap back on the bottle before he cleared his throat.

Tyrone jumped.

"Didn't mean to startle you," Gerard said. "I'm sorry for your loss. Drowned in her bathtub, I understand. Terrible thing."

Tyrone was wary, probably took him for a narc.

"I'm a big fan of your mother's," Gerard said. "Seen all her films. On Turner Classic Movies, of course. I'm much too young to have seen them on release." He indicated the church. "Big turnout. Lavish event. Specified in the will, I suspect. Even the most devoted son would choke on the cost."

Tyrone frowned. "What are you talking about?"

"I did my college dissertation on the deaths of movie stars," Gerard said. He was, of course, making it up out of whole cloth. "Your mother hung around too long to make the cut, but I studied her at the time."

Tyrone's head was coming off. "Look, I need to get back."

"Satisfy my curiosity first. A movie star of her age, richer than God. Usually they don't leave it to family—they hold a grudge for some imagined slight, leave it to charity instead, usually with their name attached. The Vanessa Morgan Grant.

The Vanessa Morgan Hospital for Special Surgery. And the cost of the funeral eats into what would be going to the heirs."

Tyrone exhaled impatiently. "Do you have a point?"

"They usually leave the stock to the family, though. That's the saving grace. Of course, it takes a while to convert stock into cash." Gerard smiled. "I imagine you'll be needing cash."

15

Mason Kimble loaded the video into Final Cut Pro. It popped up in the directory as Untitled. He double-clicked on it, and the footage appeared in the preview screen.

"How much are you going to use?" Gerard Cardigan said.

"Just a clip, a teaser. Enough to prove we have footage she wouldn't want going public. A good clip, though."

Mason clicked Play and they watched the video of Tessa Tweed again. He stopped it on the money shot, backed up a few seconds, and marked the clip. Then he ran it forward a few seconds past the spot where he'd stopped before, and marked the clip again. He clicked on the section he'd marked, and that short segment jumped down into the timeline of the film. He clicked on that and played the segment in the viewer screen.

"And that's it," he said. He loaded a blank disc into the computer and copied the clip. "Now we play that back to make sure it transferred." He ejected the disc, fed it into a DVD player, and played it back. "Beautiful."

He ejected the disc, wiped any fingerprints off it, and slipped it into a white paper sleeve.

"Now we delete this entire project from Final Cut Pro without saving it, and it's as if it's never been here."

Mason deleted the project. He picked up the disc. "And we are left with this marvelous preview of coming attractions." He slipped the disc sleeve into a padded manila envelope. Then from a plastic shopping bag on his desk, he removed a brand-new cell phone, wiped it clean, and put it in, too. "Now, there's a pretty package." Mason extended it to Gerard. "Would you be so good as to see that the young lady gets it?"

"Do you want to put her name on it?"

Mason smiled. "Oh, she'll know who it's for."

16

Tessa Tweed was feeling good. The scene she'd just filmed with Brad had gone superbly. It was sensational, an emotionally charged tour de force that was the spine of the picture. The type of scene that makes or breaks a movie.

Brad, for once, had stepped up. He'd forgotten he was acting, and let her lead him along. The result was one of the finest scenes shot on a soundstage in a long, long time. The crew had actually applauded.

Tessa skipped up the steps of her trailer, giddy in the elation of the moment.

Just inside the door was a padded manila envelope. There was nothing written on it, so it might have been dropped there by a production assistant, but Tessa didn't think so.

Tessa snatched up the envelope and found it heavier than she expected. She sat in a chair in her kitchen nook and dumped the contents of the envelope out on the tabletop.

It was a cell phone and a DVD.

Tessa picked up the cell phone.

It rang.

Tessa was so startled she dropped it. She reached out to grab it, but hesitated.

Whoever had sent the phone was watching.

She ducked down out of view and approached the window. She carefully flicked the curtain to the side and peeked out, but could see nothing suspicious, just the typical activity on the lot. Nobody who seemed out of place or who appeared to be watching her trailer, but with so many people milling around in a constant flurry of activity, it was hard to tell.

The phone rang again. She snatched it up and pressed the green icon accepting the call. "Hello?"

"Hello, Tessa."

"Who is this?"

"You know who this is, and you know what I want."

"No, I don't."

"I'm the man who sent you the phone."

"Yes, but . . . "

"But what? That's all you need to know. I sent you the phone, and you're going to do exactly what I say."

"No, I'm not."

"Don't be hasty. Play the video," Mason said, and hung up.

Tessa had a flat-screen TV mounted to her wall, connected to a Blu-ray player concealed in a cabinet.

She opened the tray on the player, put in the disc, and pressed Close.

The player roared to life, and an arrow filled the screen. Tessa picked up the remote and pressed Play.

It was worse than she'd thought. Tessa sank down in her chair and buried her head in her hands.

17

Tessa pulled Teddy into her trailer. One look at her face told him all he needed to know.

"Another letter?"

"Worse."

"In what way?"

"A cell phone and a DVD."

"How were they delivered?"

"A padded manila envelope left inside my trailer door."

"Anything written on it?"

"No."

"Any note inside?"

"No, but the cell phone rang as soon as I took it out."

"Really?" Teddy said casually, but that concerned him. The man would have had to be watching the trailer to know when to call. A blackmailer was bad enough, but a stalker was something else. "What did he say?"

"He said, 'I'm the man who sent you the phone and you're going to do exactly what I say.' I told him I wasn't, and he told me to 'play the video.' So I did. It was awful. The photo was almost benign, just a hint of what they might have. But the video . . ."

"Did they send the whole tape?"

"Just a few seconds, but that was enough. It was so . . . revealing." Tessa shivered. "I felt violated."

"Well, there's a silver lining. The man was a potential danger, but you didn't know how much. Now he's shot his bolt and revealed his leverage. He's got nothing more."

"Are you crazy? He can make it public."

"He's not going to do that. Where's the cell phone?"

Tessa pointed to the kitchen table. "That's it."

Teddy slipped it into his pocket.

"What if he tries to call me again?"

"He won't, at least not on that phone. He still hasn't asked you for anything. At the moment he's just getting off on scaring you, manipulating you, making you think you're in his power. That's all this is about. Dominance."

Tessa shuddered again. She took a breath. "At least . . ."

"At least what?"

"It wasn't Nigel."

"What?"

"Now I've heard his voice. And it wasn't Nigel."

"Right," Teddy said, but he didn't buy it for a moment. Nigel might not be the voice on the phone, but he could still be behind this. In any case, he was the source of the video.

Despite what Tessa might think, Teddy planned to set his sights on Nigel.

18

Teddy called Mike Freeman at Strategic Services. Mike knew Teddy's background and had once offered him a job. The offer was always open.

"Hi, Mike. It's Billy Barnett."

"Oh, is it now?"

"What's that supposed to mean?"

"I understand you're a movie star these days."

"How do you understand that?"

"I have a widespread network of surveillance equipment and personnel, and I like to keep tabs on you. I might need you someday."

"Or vice versa."

"What are you saying?"

"A little matter's come up. I could use your assistance."

"*My* assistance?"

"Well, the assistance of your widespread network of surveillance equipment and personnel. I'm looking for a young man by the name of Nigel Hightower the Third, reportedly here in L.A."

"You can't find him yourself?"

"Hey, I'm a movie star. I've got my hands full."

"Ah, the price of fame."

"Fuck you, Mike. I'm one guy juggling multiple identities and trying to help Peter Barrington make a picture. This Hightower thing is a favor for a friend. It's important, and I need it done fast."

"My firm's in New York. You think I'm the best man for the job?"

"I know you are."

"You want to tell me why this is so important?"

"No."

"Suit yourself. Say hi to Peter for me."

"I won't be telling him."

"It's like that, is it?"

"Don't jump to any conclusions."

"I never do."

"Call me as soon as you find him."

"What makes you think we will?"

"I have a gut feeling."

19

Teddy was crouching on a ledge outside a fourteenth-story hotel room window when Mike called back. Luckily his cell phone was on vibrate or he might have ruined the shot. He was also lucky they were filming on the soundstage on the back lot of Centurion Studios and he wasn't the main focus. The ledge he was crouching on was part of the set they had built to shoot the hotel room scene between Tessa and Brad. Teddy was literally window dressing. He could occasionally be seen in the background ducking down in the window if Brad or Tessa came his way. The actual scene of Teddy on the ledge, plus his perilous climb to get there, would be filmed on location on the fourteenth floor of a hotel in downtown L.A. A call during the sequence would have been really inconvenient.

Teddy called back while Peter was giving notes between takes. Peter always gave notes between takes. Brad was the type of actor who needed notes.

"What's up, Mike?"

"A young man answering the description of Nigel High-tower the Third has a habit of getting high on coke and leaving most if not all of his bankroll in an illegal hold 'em club in Chinatown."

"How'd you find that out?"

"You don't want to know."

"I'm paying for it."

"That's why you don't."

"Now you've made me suspicious, Mike. What's going on?"

"My men are out canvassing, touching base with their informants, and a hooker happened to recognize him. She said the kid had paid for her company of an evening, but was so high on coke he couldn't cut the mustard, if you know what I mean."

"Where did the hooker make the acquaintance of this young man?"

"At an underground club—both figuratively and literally. Ringtone Lee's place, in the basement under a noodle shop."

"'Ringtone'?"

"I assume it's a nickname, but apparently there is such a guy. Anyway, we got him. Nigel plays every Friday night. I'll put triple coverage on him and follow him home."

"No," Teddy said.

Mike was surprised. "No?"

"Don't follow him home. Pull everybody off him. When he leaves that club, I don't want an agent anywhere near the place."

"Uh-oh," Mike said.

20

Nigel Hightower III was winning, which was not unusual. Nigel often won in the beginning, before flushing his entire wad of cash on an ill-considered bet. But tonight he'd been winning steadily for hours, and built his original stack of two thousand dollars up to five. Visions of moving into more desirable living quarters danced in his head. Sure, he owed the landlord six months' rent, but that was under the name of Harvey Wilson, and if that notable deadbeat were to skip town, who would even think twice about it? He'd be able to afford fifteen hundred bucks for a sham ID and credit rating, and he could make a new start. After all, didn't everyone deserve a new start?

Nigel hit pocket threes and limped into the pot. If he hit on the flop he could clean up; if he missed, all he lost was the big blind. The game was dollar, two, no-limit, so he was basically risking two dollars for the chance to mint money.

Nigel hit a third three on the flop. He checked, slow-playing the hand, cunningly lying in wait for the money to come in.

It did. Two players bet up the pot. One folded after the turn.

The other guy, who had just bought into the game with a huge stack, made a big bet on the river.

Nigel went all in and he called.

The son of a bitch had a straight.

Nigel had him covered, which meant he had more money than his opponent, but not much. After paying him off, Nigel had only a hundred and eighty dollars left. He could have kept playing, but it had taken him a long time to build up his stack, and a hundred and eighty dollars was hardly enough to buy in. Not when he was angry enough to shove it on the first hand.

Nigel knew better than to make a scene. It was not done. If you lost, it was no one's fault, just the luck of the draw. You accepted the outcome, or you didn't come back. Nigel remembered the schmuck who had lost five hundred dollars on a single hand and had smashed a glass. Ringtone Lee's bouncer didn't look like much, but the man was fast. The asshole was out the door before he knew what hit him.

So even with the nagging suspicion in his mind that Ringtone Lee had sent the guy who won the pot into the game to take him down, Nigel wasn't about to complain. It didn't matter. Nigel was playing great and a high roller was just another chance to double his chips.

Or lose them all.

The bouncer led Nigel out and walked him up the long, narrow stairs to the street. The basement steps would have been heaven for muggers, who might be waiting outside the battered metal door. Not that players leaving Ringtone Lee's often had much money, but even so.

Tonight there were no muggers to shoo away. The bouncer took a look around the back lot where the players' cars were parked, and went back in.

Nigel dug his keys out of his pocket. Now that he was alone, the only thing that kept him from flipping out entirely was the thought that there might be surveillance cameras in the lot.

There weren't. Teddy Fay had checked that out. There were no cameras, no guard, no security system of any type.

When Nigel opened the door of his car, Teddy stepped up and plunged a hypodermic needle into his neck.

21

Nigel came to on the floor. It was moving and bumping somewhat, which was what had jostled him awake. Groggy and disoriented, he blinked and opened his eyes.

Teddy was sitting in a seat looking down at him. "Well, well. Look who decided to join the party."

"Where am I?"

Teddy shrugged. "I have no idea. That's the thing with auto-pilot. You don't really have to pay attention."

"Huh?"

"You're in a private jet. I can't tell you exactly where you are, but you're flying at fifteen thousand feet at five hundred miles per hour. Do you know what happens when you open the cabin door at that speed? More to the point, do you know what happens when a person plummets to the earth from a height of over two miles? Neither do I. Colleges are strict about grant money, and it's hard to get volunteers. However, it goes by rather quickly. You can calculate it by the formula for falling objects, though the odds are by the time you reach a solution it will no longer be of any use to you."

"What do you want?"

"What's your name?"

"Nigel Hightower."

"What do you do, Nigel?"

"I'm an investor."

Teddy scoffed. "An investor? You're a rich prick. You spend what Daddy gives you and hustle the rest."

"Now, see here—"

"Did you go to Oxford?"

"Yes."

"You knew Tessa Tweed?"

"Oh."

"You're a real schmuck, aren't you? Filmed your girlfriend without her knowledge. I suppose you saw that as a harmless prank. Then you told her you destroyed it, but you kept a copy. I suppose that was just for you to look at. At least at first, until she became famous. Then you started showing it around."

"No."

"No? Then I wonder what we're doing here. I take it you aren't the one using the tape to pressure her?"

"No!"

"Who is?"

"I don't know."

"But you do. He's got that tape, and you're the only source. At least I *hope* you're the only source . . . or did you share it with anyone else?"

"No, no, of course not."

"Then it had to have come from you. Damned by your own ethics. Strange word to apply to you. Ethics. Have you got any ethics, Nigel? You had a girlfriend in college who's a film star now, who you can't help bragging about. You wouldn't blackmail her with that film, would you?"

"Of course not."

"But you'd let someone else do it."

"No, I—"

"You're a loser, Nigel, and you've always been a loser. A loser needs a stake. A guy says to you, 'You give me that tape, I'll give you twenty thousand dollars. You don't give me that tape, I'll break your thumbs.' Well, your thumbs aren't broken, Nigel. What do you have to say for yourself?"

"Ten thousand."

"What?"

"It was only ten thousand."

"Who gave you the money?"

"I tell you, I don't know."

"You've told me a lot of things, Nigel, and some of them might be true. With you it's hard to tell. So, last chance to stay in the plane. I want a name. Give me a name, Nigel."

Nigel looked like he was about to cry. "I don't know."

"What did the guy look like?"

"There's no guy," Nigel cried.

"Then you're the guy, Nigel. If there's no guy, you're him."

"There's a guy," Nigel said. "I never met him. I came back to the car and there was a manila envelope on the front seat. I don't know how, the car was locked, but there it was. There was a thousand bucks inside, and a note."

"What did it say?"

"I still have it." Nigel scrunched around on the plane floor and dug into his hip pocket. He pulled out a folded paper. He unfolded it and read, "'Use this thousand to play tomorrow night. Leave this manila envelope with the video on the front seat. When you cash out, the video will be gone, and you will find another nine thousand in the envelope. If you do not comply with these instructions, I will assume you have stolen one thousand dollars from me, and act accordingly. Leaving the money in the envelope would not relieve you of your obligation. I will assume you are taunting me with your stolen goods, and act accordingly.'"

"You did what the letter said?"

"Wouldn't you?"

"I find it hard to put myself in the position of someone who would have abused his girlfriend in the first place. Tell me, was this the same night you were shooting your mouth off around the club?"

"I didn't say I was shooting my mouth off around the club."

"You did, though, didn't you? Because you were nursing a bad loss and you wanted to make yourself feel better. So you said, 'Well, I may not be lucky in cards, but guess what?'"

"How do you know what I said?"

"Because you're not as cool as you think you are, even for a loser." Teddy cocked his head. "Well, it would appear you are of no further use to me. I'm going back to the cockpit to strap myself in. The plane tends to buck around a little when the cabin door's open."

Nigel was frantic. "Wait! Wait!"

"What?"

"I told you what you wanted to know."

"Yes."

"So you're going to let me go."

Teddy pretended to consider. "Okay, here's what you're going to do. You're never going to mention the video again. If you have any copies, you're going to destroy them. You're not going back to the hold 'em club. In fact, you're going to leave town, and you're not coming back until I clean up this mess you created. You can give me your cell phone number, and I'll let you know. Do we have a deal?"

Nigel nodded his head vigorously.

Teddy shrugged. "Too bad." He gestured to the door. "You could have joined the mile-high club."

22

Teddy dressed himself up as an asshole, a rich old guy trying to make himself look cool with long hair and casual clothes, but whose two-thousand-dollar corduroy jacket sort of gave the thing away. So did the Mercedes-Benz he borrowed off the Centurion back lot.

Teddy parked behind the noodle shop and rang the bell beside the battered iron door to the basement. Ringtone Lee's bouncer pushed the door open a minute later. His look was not welcoming.

Teddy stuffed two hundreds into his hand and said, "Get me a seat at the table."

The bouncer considered that. The money disappeared into his pocket. He turned Teddy around and patted him down for a weapon. Finding none, he said, "You got cash?"

Teddy jerked his thumb at the guy's pocket. "That was sort of a hint."

"If you're a wise guy, we don't want you."

Teddy jerked a wad of cash out of his pants pocket. "You want me."

There were seven guys already at the table. Teddy sat down and made eight. He began to lose, which wasn't easy, as they weren't very good.

Teddy called the pot with a hand he knew would lose and cursed his luck. "Not my night. I should have gone out instead—I could have gotten laid."

"Yeah, sure," the guy across the table from him said. He was a snotty son of a bitch, snide to everybody. Teddy would have loved to take him down. But he wasn't Teddy's target.

The guy he wanted was the little guy to his right whose ears pricked up when Teddy said, "You wouldn't believe who I'm going out with."

"She got two legs or four?" the snotty guy said.

Teddy didn't answer, just let the matter drop.

The little man bit. "So who is it?"

"An absolute knockout. You might recognize her."

"She's famous?"

"She's done lingerie ads."

"Oh. So I wouldn't recognize her name?"

"Maybe not."

"You're saying I might recognize her face?"

"Among other things," the snotty guy said.

The little guy lost interest. He also lost money. Teddy busted him, which wasn't hard. He sucked him in, set him up. The guy didn't have much to begin with, but after Teddy began to work on him his pile went fast. He lost all his chips and cashed out.

So did Teddy. The other players couldn't believe he was leaving. He hadn't been there that long.

"You win one pot and walk away," the snide guy said. "I can't stand players like that. Quit as soon as they're up, and say they won. You gonna go brag about it?"

Teddy wished he had time to knock him down a peg.

Teddy caught the little man in the parking lot. He was surprised to see Teddy. "You cashed out, too?"

"I came out to give you back your money."

The little guy was dumbfounded. "What?"

"I felt bad taking it. You're a terrible player, you must lose all the time. I figure you must have another source of income."

"Now, see here—"

"Of course, if you're too proud to accept the money, I quite understand, but you and I are going to have a little talk."

"No, we're not."

"Oh yes, we are," Teddy said. "Now, they patted me down for a weapon, but I don't really need one, do I?"

The little man's mind was totally blown. He blinked at Teddy.

"You perked up at my dating-a-celebrity story like you just caught aces in the hole. And your disappointment when it wasn't worth shit was almost comical. You were hoping it was something you could turn a profit with. Like that British kid who once dated a movie star."

Once again, the little guy's face betrayed him.

"See, that's why you're such a bad player," Teddy said. "You have a million tells. So who'd you sell the info to? And don't be coy. One way or another, you're going to tell me."

"There's a private eye I pass tips on to. If one pans out, he slips me money."

"I thought there might be. What's his name?"

"Ace Vargas."

"Ace?" Teddy said. "Is his name really Ace?"

"Sure. Ace Detective Agency."

"You told him about this kid?"

"That's right."

"You told him the kid's name?"

"I didn't have his name."

"Remarkable. Another tell. You gave him the name of the movie star. Who was it?"

"Tessa Tweed."

"Uh-huh. And why was this information worth so much money?"

"It just was."

"Bullshit. That nugget isn't worth a dime. What else did the kid tell you that made it worthwhile?"

"He said he filmed himself with her."

"Having sex?"

"Yeah."

"And that's what you told your detective friend?"

"Yeah."

"You didn't see the tape?"

"No."

"The kid wasn't flashing around a copy?"

"He didn't have it with him or he might have. It seemed important to him that we believe him."

"You better be on the up-and-up about this Ace Vargas."

"I swear."

"If you're not, believe me, I will find you." Teddy shoved the money into his hands. "Go back, play cards, and forget you ever met me. You get a mulligan on the game. It's not often you get a do-over on your whole day."

Teddy figured it was a fifty-fifty chance the guy would tip Ace off, but it didn't matter. A PI with an agency would have no place to hide.

Teddy went home and went to bed. They were filming the next day, and he had a six AM call.

23

The other players were surprised to see the little man again.

"I thought you went bust," the snide guy said.

"I went to get cash. I'm buying in again, as soon as I go to the john."

The little man went in the bathroom and locked the door. He whipped out his cell phone and brought up his contact screen, and he clicked on Ace. There were two numbers listed, his office and his home number. He often got leads after hours and the detective didn't want to wait.

Of course he didn't usually call him at two AM.

Ace was groggy and pissed. "Listen, dipshit, this better be good."

"It's a hot tip, but it isn't good. I'm calling to warn you. There's a guy on your tail. I think he's private."

"You think?"

"He showed up at the club posing as a rube. Cleaned me out

and confronted me in the parking lot. He's after the Tessa Tweed video."

"You gave him my name?"

"He would have killed me. I had no choice. He told me not to warn you, but I am."

"What does he look like?"

"Long hair, dressed like a hippie, but he's not. Twenty bucks it's just for effect."

"Did you give him my home address?"

"I didn't give him any address. I said you ran the Ace Detective Agency. He'll come during business hours, assuming he comes at all."

"All right. Call me if you hear anything."

Ace hung up and called Mason Kimble. Ace had done a couple of jobs for Mason and knew he was interested in Centurion Pictures. A scandal involving one of their leading actresses figured to be a juicy tidbit, particularly one involving the wife of the head of the studio. Ace had been right. Mason had paid and paid well. He'd want a heads-up about this new development. And he'd pay for that, too.

Mason was disoriented. "What the hell time is it?"

"It's two in the morning. Sorry to call you, but it's important. This is Ace Vargas. There's a private dick looking for the Tessa Tweed tape."

Mason was suddenly awake. "Really? Did he talk to you?"

"No, but he's on his way. Probably tomorrow during working hours. I'll keep your name out of it, but I'm going to take a pounding, and I may need compensation."

"Come in to work an hour early, I'll send you some cash. I don't want my man to cross paths with this guy."

"You got it."

M ason hung up and called Gerard Cardigan. Gerard processed the information with his usual understated aplomb. "That's unfortunate," he said.

"It is," Mason said.

"Would you like me to handle it?"

"I would."

"Don't give it another thought."

"It has to be done early, before this detective gets there."

"How early?"

"Vargas will be there at eight."

"So will I," Gerard said.

24

Teddy had an early call, so there was no chance of swinging by the Ace Detective Agency before work. He went to the studio, got into costume and makeup, and prepared to shoot his scene. While he waited he called the agency to see if Ace Vargas had come in early, but there was no answer. Teddy kept calling every ten minutes or so. Finally, around eight-fifteen, someone answered, "Hello?"

Teddy hung up. He didn't want to talk to Ace on the phone, he wanted to talk to him in person. Now that he knew Ace was there, he'd run over the first chance he got.

Only he never got a chance. Teddy was tied up on the set all morning. Peter was shooting close-ups and reverse angles for a scene for which he'd already shot the master, so the action was locked, and there was nothing new. Teddy knew Peter needed the footage to cut the scene, but he chafed at the delay.

Teddy was killing a hotel bellboy when Tessa showed up. The bellboy hadn't done anything except see Teddy come out of the wrong hotel room, but that was his tough luck. He'd be found in a linen closet later on.

Teddy had his hands around the unfortunate man's throat when Tessa walked in. He continued to kill him until Peter called, "Cut!"

Tessa pulled Teddy aside while Peter reset the scene. Apparently the young bellboy was going to die again.

"You look worried," Tessa said.

"I'm not."

Tessa didn't buy it. "Are you making any progress?"

"Some."

"You don't want to tell me?"

"I'll tell you when it matters."

"Okay, but can you tell me this? It isn't Nigel, is it?"

"Nigel's not the one behind the blackmail, but he *was* the source of the tape. He sold it to pay off his gambling debts."

"I don't believe it."

"He's a bad gambler. Some people are, and Nigel's worse than most."

"Who did he sell it to?"

"That's what I'm working on."

"Any progress?"

Teddy shook his head. "You don't take no for an answer, do you?"

"I know you haven't found who sent the video. But you have a lead, don't you?"

"I have a lead. It isn't much."

"How much?"

Teddy sighed. "Pretty damn little. The Ace Detective Agency

may have acted as an intermediary. I'm going to shake them down during lunch."

"They're in L.A.?"

"Yes."

"So Nigel's in L.A.?"

"He's not in L.A."

"Are you positive?"

"Oh, yeah."

"How can you be sure?"

Teddy smiled. He had an image of Nigel cowering on the floor of his jet, expecting at any moment to go hurtling out the cabin door.

"Just a hunch."

25

When Peter broke for lunch, Teddy walked off the lot and got his car. As producer Billy Barnett, he had a parking space, but as stuntman Mark Weldon, he didn't rate such special treatment, and never would until his name appeared above the title. That'll be the day, he told himself.

Teddy drove downtown to the Ace Detective Agency. He parked two blocks away and walked to the address.

It was an old office building, with the accent on *old*. The elevator looked iffy, so Teddy took the stairs up to the third floor and looked for the Ace Detective Agency. It wasn't hard to find. The door had a frosted glass window with ACE DETECTIVE AGENCY stenciled on it, just like in the movies.

Teddy banged on the door to no avail. He sighed, fished a couple of picks out of his pocket, and jimmied the lock. The door clicked open.

The Ace Detective Agency wasn't as prosperous as the ones in old films, with an attractive dame manning a switchboard in the outer office. In fact, it had no outer office at all. It was a small, one-room affair, with overflowing file cabinets, a couple of folding chairs, an ancient computer, and a single metal desk.

Ace Vargas sat behind the desk, but he could be excused for not answering the door. Ace had been shot in the head.

Teddy had few options, none of them good. He could call the police and wait for them to arrive. He could call the police and get the hell out of there. Or he could get the hell out of there and not call the police.

The third option seemed best.

Teddy slipped out the office door and checked the hall. There was a surveillance camera right outside the detective agency. A wire from it ran across the ceiling to the corner, then down and into the floor. The recording equipment was in either a guard station or the basement. Teddy doubted the building had ever been well-to-do enough to merit a guard station, so he took the stairs down to the lobby, pushed through a service door, and found the cellar stairs. At the bottom of the stairs was a depressing jumble of steam pipes on which the asbestos covers were flaking off. A storeroom had a relatively new-looking padlock on it. Teddy picked the lock and pulled the string of a hanging bare bulb.

A battered old metal desk held a TV monitor, old and big and bulky with a dozen split-screen images of interior views of the building. Next to the monitor was a VCR of similar vintage, a monstrous affair with slots for twelve VHS tapes. All were recording. The VCR appeared to be set to record for six hours until it reached the end of the tape, then automatically rewind and start recording from the beginning. It was a most inefficient system. Any crime committed more than six hours ago would be gone.

If Ace had been killed within the last six hours, the killer might be on the tapes. Unfortunately, Teddy would be, too.

Teddy had no time to look. He ejected all the tapes, found an old paper bag, and threw them in.

He went out to his car and locked the tapes in the trunk, then retrieved a pair of plastic gloves, went back into the building, and searched the office. He turned it upside down to make sure Ace hadn't kept a copy of the video. It was the type of thing a private eye of Ace's ilk would be apt to do, but there was no sign of it.

Teddy found nothing of interest. The office files were all old, and probably left by the previous tenant. The computer had nothing as useful as a Quicken account with labeled deposits or current e-mails of any note.

Teddy figured he'd pressed his luck far enough. He wiped everything down and got out.

Teddy hopped in his car and sped to his house. He popped the trunk, grabbed the bag of tapes, went in and locked it in his floor safe.

He raced back to the car and took off. He was late. He floored it, trying to make up time.

As he approached the studio, he skidded into a turn and hurtled through the Centurion Studios gate onto the back lot.

Teddy checked his watch. Two minutes to go. He pulled into Brad's parking space, leaped out of the car, and came strolling casually onto the set as if he'd been there all along.

26

Tessa pounced on Teddy as soon as he walked onto the set. "Did you see the detective?"

"In a manner of speaking."

"What do you mean?"

Peter was still setting up camera angles. Teddy motioned Tessa away from the set. "Come on. Let's rehearse our lines."

"Our lines?"

"Come on."

Teddy led her over to the coffee urn. He poured them each a cup, then walked her out of earshot as a couple of grips wandered over for coffee.

"Okay," Teddy said. "We're going to find out how good an actress you are."

"What?"

"You're going to have to go on the set and act like nothing happened."

"What are you talking about?"

"I was unable to meet with Ace Vargas this afternoon

because someone went up to his office this morning and shot him in the head."

"What!"

"The police don't know it yet, and it's rather important not to give anyone the impression that you knew it before they do. Hence the acting."

"Then why are you telling me this?"

"I'm telling you this because you didn't have a morning call. You just came by the set to pump me for information, because you're desperate, and desperation leads to bad decisions. I want to make sure you won't do anything rash. You must trust me. The situation has become deadly, and I need you out of the line of fire. If I'm worrying about you, I can't focus on solving the problem. Will you promise me to stay out of this? To let me handle it?"

Tessa looked chastened. "You have my word."

From the direction of the set came the exasperated voice of Brad Hunter. "Hey! Who parked in my spot?"

27

eddy's scenes wrapped early. Peter shot the Teddy and Tessa scene first, and the rest of the afternoon was just Tessa and Brad.

He went home and removed the videotapes from the safe. If the surveillance camera was working, they might show the killer, and him.

In order to watch them, Teddy had to buy a VCR, which wasn't easy. No one used them anymore. He found one in a pawnshop for twenty dollars.

"Do you have a tape I can try?" Teddy asked.

The pawnbroker was exasperated. "Are you shitting me? You're not buying a home entertainment system. Twenty bucks, as is. I'll throw in the cables."

Teddy took it home and hooked it up to his TV. The remote didn't work, no big surprise. Teddy replaced the batteries, pressed the power button, and the machine clicked on.

The first tape he tried was all static. Teddy couldn't tell if that was the tape, or if the player didn't work. He took the tape out and tried another. He rewound slightly and pressed Play, with the same result. A third tape was no better.

Teddy considered running out to one of those mall stores where they had bins of old prerecorded tapes for $2.99 to test the machine. It was a depressing prospect.

The VCR made a clacking sound. It had rewound to the beginning of the tape and shut off.

Teddy pressed Play.

An image filled the screen. It was a hallway in the building, but not the one outside the Ace Detective Agency. Teddy could make out the office number 810.

Teddy held down the fast forward button and the images jumped across the screen. At least they would have, if anything had been happening. The scene was just an empty hallway.

Teddy stopped the tape, hit fast forward again, and wound ahead. After several seconds he stopped the tape and pressed Play. The image was the same.

Teddy kept running the tape forward until static filled the screen. He ejected the tape and saw that it had stopped right about in the middle. It was rewound slightly farther than the other tapes from the machine.

Using the tape as a guide, he rewound another tape slightly past that spot. Another view from the building appeared, this one from a back staircase. Teddy located the spot where the image became static. It was exactly the same place as on the other tape. Teddy tried another tape with the same results.

That confirmed the hypothesis. The killer would not appear

on any of the tapes. Nor would he. The killer hadn't just disabled the camera on the third floor, he'd cut the main feed before going in.

Teddy couldn't help but feel a grudging admiration.

This guy was good.

28

Mason Kimble leaned back in his desk chair, luxuriating in his power. "Pass me a bubble-wrap mailer, will you?"

Gerard Cardigan got up and went to the short bookshelf that served as the company mail station. He took a mailer off the pile and brought it back for Mason. "Do you have a special delivery for our friend?"

"I do."

"How much of the video are you going to send her?"

Mason smiled. "I'm not sending her the video."

"Oh? What are you sending her?"

"You know perfectly well what I'm sending her. You knew as soon as I asked you to hang on to it."

"I suspected. I didn't know for sure."

"Now you do."

"She won't know what it is."

"It doesn't matter. It will frighten her."

"That it will," Gerard said. "Do you want me to drop it off in the morning?"

Mason smiled. "Why wait?"

29

The doorbell rang at two AM. Tessa heard it and hopped out of bed. She had been tossing and turning all night, keyed up from Teddy's news and his caution to her.

Ben slept through the bell. It was a single chime, discreet, tasteful, nearly inaudible. Ben had complained about it, saying they'd miss someone because they couldn't hear the door. Tessa said that would never happen. Ben had pointed out, how would she possibly know?

Tessa peered out the window to see who it was. She prayed it wouldn't be a man she didn't know. If it was, she couldn't let him in, but she was terrified of what would happen if she didn't.

There was no one there.

Somehow, that was even more frightening.

Tessa eased the door open a crack, prepared to slam it if someone was lurking in the shadows, but no one was. She opened the door wider, hoping against hope there wouldn't be a padded mailer on her doorstep. There was. She snatched it up and swayed for a moment, afraid to bring it in the house and afraid to leave it out in the open. What could it be this time? Somehow she just knew it would be worse. It was heavier, if that meant anything.

She took it into the kitchen and switched the light on.

Tessa reached into the mailer and pulled out the cold metal object.

It was a gun.

Teddy groped for his cell phone and clicked it on. "Somebody better be dead, or someone will be."

"I'm sorry," Tessa whispered urgently. "I need your help."

"Where are you?"

"I'm at home."

"Then you're safe. I'll talk to you in the morning."

"No, wait! Someone delivered a gun to my front door!"

"When?"

"Just now. The doorbell rang. I went to the door, and on the porch was a bubble-wrap mailer. I think it's the murder weapon."

"What makes you think that?"

"It's been fired recently."

"What do you know about guns?"

"Back home I used to target-shoot on a private estate. The gun is a revolver. It's fully loaded, but there's an empty shell in one of the chambers."

"Shit."

"What should I do?"

"Is Ben up?"

"He slept right through the doorbell. Nothing wakes him."

"Hang on. I'll be right there."

"You can't come by at two in the morning."

"I'm not coming in. I'll be there in ten minutes. Be watching out the window. When you see the car, leave the mailer with the gun inside on the stoop."

Teddy hurriedly pulled on some clothes. He grabbed his keys and wallet, slipped on a pair of sneakers, and hopped in the car. He observed the speed laws on his way. That time of night a lone car speeding would attract attention.

Ben and Tessa lived in a Hollywood home with an inordinate amount of lawn. Teddy left the car on the street and sprinted up the drive in his unlaced sneakers. He saw the front door open, and a shadowy figure place the mailer on the stoop.

Teddy picked up the mailer with the gun and slipped off the path into the darkness. He stood stock-still, listening for a sound but heard none. He worked his way quickly around the perimeter of the property to the street.

No one seemed to be watching his car, but that didn't mean someone wasn't. There was no help for that now. Teddy got in, started the engine, and pulled away. He drove the speed limit all the way home.

He parked in his driveway, hurried up the walk, and went inside. It was a relief to get home, but he didn't relax until he'd locked the gun in his safe.

30

A local newscast reported the murder of private detective Ace Vargas. Teddy had planned on ignoring the case altogether, but that was before he was in possession of a recently fired gun that was likely the murder weapon.

He disguised himself as Jonathan Foster, one of several identities for whom he had CIA credentials. Foster was a little younger than Teddy, but looked like a seasoned pro. Teddy checked his image in the mirror against the ID photo. It was close enough. He got in his car and drove into downtown L.A.

Teddy went to the police station and hunted up the detective in charge of the Ace Vargas case. He was lucky to find him in his office. Sergeant Marvin O'Reilly was a beefy middle-aged cop with a firm handshake.

"Oh, thank God," Teddy said.

The sergeant frowned. "I beg your pardon?"

"I was afraid I'd get some twenty-year-old kid who doesn't know the ropes."

O'Reilly almost smiled. "What's this all about?"

Teddy whipped out his credentials. "Jonathan Foster, CIA. A matter has arisen with regard to the Ace Vargas case."

The sergeant scowled.

Teddy put up his hands. "Don't worry, we're not taking over the investigation. I'm not here to step on your toes. We have one small matter, totally incidental to your case, and I'm here to see it stays that way." He took a breath. "Now then, I can't tell you much—this is all highly classified—but we have reason to believe that the fatal gun in the Ace Vargas case may have been used in one other unrelated homicide."

"We don't *have* the fatal gun in the Ace Vargas case."

"No, but you've got the fatal bullet."

O'Reilly frowned. "I can't give you the fatal bullet."

"No, but you can give me a ballistics photo. We can work from that. It's not as accurate, but good enough for our purposes. We're not trying to prove something in court."

"You want the ballistics photo?"

"Surely you have copies."

O'Reilly frowned. "I don't know."

"You're in charge of the case, right?"

"Yeah."

"You haven't made an arrest yet, have you?"

"No," O'Reilly said with an edge in his voice.

"Good."

He frowned again. "Why do you say that?"

Teddy shrugged. "The minute you make an arrest, the assistant district attorney is in charge of the case. Those guys are assholes."

Fifteen minutes later Teddy was out the door with a copy of the ballistics photo.

T eddy went home and logged into the CIA website. It took him fifteen minutes to get into the encrypted and encoded classified section. They kept changing the codes to keep him out. Of course, they had no idea when he got in, they just took the precaution as a matter of course.

This time Teddy wasn't looking for any classified information, just the kind of info that wasn't available to the general public. Like the names and locations of CIA agents around the globe.

Teddy was particularly concerned with the L.A. area. He had a feeling there might be a local office set up to monitor suspected terrorist activity on college campuses. There was indeed. It covered all of southern California and boasted a director, half a dozen in-house personnel, and seventeen field agents. Files were available on all.

Teddy chose Jaspar Billingham—young, eager, ambitious, one of two agents currently doubling as armorers and lab technicians. Reading between the lines, Teddy could tell Jaspar was eager to be out in the field.

While he was there, Teddy uploaded Jonathan Foster's CIA file onto the website. An L.A. cop wouldn't have been able to check Foster's credentials on the CIA website, but a CIA agent would.

When he was done, Teddy took the gun from his safe and sealed it in a plastic evidence envelope. He took the ballistics photo of the bullet from the Ace Vargas murder and cut off anything that indicated what it was or where it came from. He put the gun and the photo in a briefcase and drove back downtown to the CIA headquarters.

Teddy was lucky in that the main office and the lab were in two separate buildings. He went up to the lab and rang the bell. The door was opened by the young agent he'd seen on the website. Jaspar Billingham was casually dressed and gave the impression of a backroom employee working hard.

"I think you have the wrong address," he said.

"I think not," Teddy said, and flipped open his CIA credentials.

Jaspar let him in and locked the door.

"Would you mind if I took another look at your credentials?" he said.

"I'd be disappointed if you didn't. Check me out thoroughly so we don't have to talk at arm's length."

Jaspar went to the computer and scanned Jonathan Foster's credentials into the machine. Moments later his CIA file popped up. Everything checked out.

Jaspar handed the credentials back. "You're from D.C.?"

"Yes."

"Why are you out here?"

"We have a delicate situation and need your assistance with some local information. We don't want it to appear that Washington is interested."

"Really?" Jaspar said.

Teddy could tell it was killing him not to ask why. "I need you to run some tests without informing your superiors. For the basis of this assignment, *I* am your superior. I don't want you to speculate on what you are being asked to do, I just want you to do it. If you do, it will be noted and remembered by the higher-ups. How equipped is your lab?"

"I would say adequately."

"Do you have a comparison microscope?"

"We do."

"Do you know how to use it?"

"Of course."

"Good." Teddy snapped open his briefcase. He took out the evidence bag with the gun and handed it to Jaspar. "Take this gun. I want you to fire a test bullet from it, and compare it to another bullet. I can't get you that bullet, but I have an evidence photo of it." Teddy handed the photo over. "Can you compare it to the bullet in this photo and tell me if it was fired from the same gun?"

"Yes."

"Good. How fast can you do it?"

Jaspar considered. "I'm not set up to fire the bullet here. By tonight?"

Teddy nodded. "Just so no one knows you're doing it."

"I understand," Jaspar said.

"Good man," Teddy said.

Jonathan Foster had done a full morning's work. Teddy went home and changed back into Mark Weldon.

31

Teddy had a two-o'clock set call. He arrived at a quarter till, and went straight to wardrobe and makeup.

Tessa was already there. She was having her eye makeup checked, which was something she usually did herself. Teddy figured she was waiting for him.

She was. She managed some stilted small talk in front of the makeup artist, and whisked him out of the room as soon as he was done.

The soundstage was abuzz with grips and electricians and cameramen setting up.

"Let's get out of here," Teddy said. He walked her out onto the back lot.

The moment they were alone Tessa said, "So, what about the gun?"

"I'm working on the gun."

"Why did he send it to me?"

"Just to frighten you, I think."

"How do you know?"

"Because nothing happened. The other obvious reason to send you the gun is to frame you for the Ace Vargas murder."

"You do think that's the gun that killed Ace Vargas?"

"I think there's a pretty good chance. But I don't think our blackmailer is actually trying to frame you with it. If he was, he could have hidden it somewhere in your home or trailer, tipped off the authorities, and policemen would have shown up at your house with a warrant. Instead he gave it right to you, and gave you time to get rid of it. He doesn't want you in the hands of the police. He wants you free to do what he wants."

"I just wish I knew what that was," Tessa fretted. "He's toying with me."

"All of this is just setting the stage, softening you up for what comes next."

"So what can it be?"

"We'll have to wait to find out."

When he got off from filming, Teddy went home and changed back into Agent Jonathan Foster. He strapped a gun to his ankle and put on a shoulder holster. He drove downtown and spent a good half hour checking out the streets around the CIA lab, just to be sure "Jonathan Foster" hadn't been found out and he wasn't walking into a trap.

When he was relatively certain the building wasn't being watched, he crossed the street and went in.

He knocked on the door to the lab with his left hand. His right hand was under his jacket on his gun.

The look on Jaspar Billingham's face told him all was well. The young man was pleased as punch. He'd found a match.

Teddy took the gun and the photo, collected the test bullets Jaspar had fired, swore him to secrecy one more time, and got the hell out of there. He felt bad for the young man, who was probably already celebrating his promotion in his head.

Teddy went home and changed out of his Jonathan Foster guise. Then he hacked into the CIA and carefully deleted any trace of Jonathan Foster from their website. He'd have to trash the identity now. It was too bad. He was kind of fond of Agent Jonathan Foster.

32

Gerard Cardigan was listening on the phone. Every now and then he would lift the receiver from his ear and mime, "Blah, blah, blah," with his other hand. He covered the mouthpiece and shook his head. "You ask a simple question and you get someone's life story." He put the phone back to his ear. "Yes, yes, that's very interesting. What I want to know is has the transfer of stocks gone through?" That question triggered another deluge of unwanted information.

Mason Kimble extended his hand and waggled his fingers. Gerard handed him the phone. Mason took it and said, "Put Cy on." A moment later he said, "Cy, Mason Kimble. I'm trying to do the math here. I need a simple number, not an explanation. How many shares of Vanessa Morgan's holdings have been transferred to my account?" Mason grabbed a pencil, turned a piece of paper around. "Uh-huh." He scribbled on the paper. "Thank you," he said, and hung up.

Mason swiveled the paper around for Gerard.

Gerard smiled. "In some ways you're scarier than I am."

"In some ways. And the winner is . . . ?"

"Forty-two point seven percent."

"Perfect," Mason said, beaming. "And Tessa Bacchetti's seven point five makes fifty point two. That calls for champagne."

Gerard looked up. "We have champagne?"

"I had a feeling about the numbers. I picked it up this morning."

Mason opened the storage cabinet behind the desk and removed an ice bucket with a bottle of champagne cooling. He popped the cork and filled a pair of flutes. He handed one to Gerard. "To Star Pictures!"

"I told you we'd make it," Gerard said.

"We cut it close. The stockholders' meeting is next week."

"It was never in doubt."

"I'd forgotten how effective your methods of persuasion are."

Gerard took a sip. "Shall we send our date an invitation?"

"Absolutely. We want to give her time to pick out a dress."

Mason went to the storage cabinet, took out a brand-new cell phone, and wiped it clean. "Hand me a mailer, will you?"

The mailer was on the stoop when Tessa stumbled out of her front door for her six-thirty call. She opened it in the limo on her way to the set. There was no note, no DVD, just the phone. She half expected it to ring, but prayed it wouldn't. What would the driver think? He'd only hear her end of the conversation, but even so.

The phone didn't ring on her way to the set. It rang in the

middle of her scene with Brad. For once it was going well. Tessa was distracted and exhausted, which pulled her performance down, and Brad stepped his up. The result was the two of them blended perfectly and the scene flowed.

Then the phone rang.

Peter was incredulous. "Who has a cell phone on set?"

He felt bad when he realized the phone was Tessa's, but he was still annoyed, particularly when she didn't just turn it off.

"I'm sorry," she said. "I have to take this." She ran off the set, away from the cast and crew. "Yes," she said quietly, when she was out of earshot.

"You kept me waiting. I don't like to be kept waiting."

"Why did you send me a gun?"

"No, no, no. You don't get to ask questions. You only answer them. Are you going to do what I say?"

Tessa said nothing.

"I have my finger on the Upload to YouTube button."

"Yes, I'm going to do what you say."

"Good."

"I want that foul thing destroyed."

"That can happen. Or it can trend number one in Google searches. It's entirely up to you. I want you to do something for me. Are you ready to do it?"

"That depends on what it is."

"Does it really? I mean, do you really think I'd make you do something you'd like less than that video?"

Tessa waited in silence.

"Here's the deal. There's a board of directors meeting coming up for Centurion Studios. You will attend, and you will vote your stock."

"I don't attend meetings. My husband has my proxy. He votes my stock."

"A proxy is voided when the stockholder appears in person, as you will do. A man representing a corporate holding company will make a motion. You will vote your shares with him."

"I won't be at the meeting."

"If you're not at the meeting, your video will go viral."

The phone clicked dead.

Tessa slapped as big a smile as she could muster on her face and hurried back to the set. "I'm sorry," she said to Peter. "My mother was seeing a doctor, but everything's all right. I've turned my phone off."

Peter knew Tessa's mother. His father, Stone Barrington, had been dating her when Tessa first came over from England to visit.

"Is it serious?"

"It could have been, but it's fine. I know she doesn't want to talk about it."

"I thought Tessa was doing remarkable work under the circumstances," Brad said.

Tessa forced a smile. Having to endure condescending faint praise from a no-talent star was almost more than she could bear. She took a breath and went back to work.

33

Teddy showed up during the next camera move. Tessa had time to drag him into her trailer and bring him up to date.

"So that's what they want," Teddy said.

"You don't seem surprised."

"I'm not. It had to be something of this nature. A few days ago I learned that Centurion stock was being bought up by several holding companies—I can't prove it, but I suspect they represent one investor interested in a hostile takeover. They can't buy your stock, but they want to force you to vote it with them."

"So what do I do? I can't attend the meeting and vote against Ben and Peter. It would be obvious something's wrong."

"Ben's a good guy. Do you think he'd hold something that happened in college against you? Being filmed without your knowledge, for goodness sakes? Just tell him what's going on."

"I can't. You didn't see the DVD they sent me. It was awful. Horrible. I can't."

"If you say so. But eventually these secrets have a way of coming out, like it or not."

Tessa looked ill at the thought.

"Have it your way," Teddy said. "Well, don't you feel better now?"

"Better?"

"You were sick to death wondering what the blackmailer wants. Now you know."

"Yes, and it's something I can't do."

"It's something you don't *think* you can do. Come on. Compared to some of the scenarios you were envisioning, this isn't that bad."

"Not that bad? What can I do? It's a no-win situation. If I show up at the meeting and vote my shares against him, Ben will want to know why. If I don't show up at the meeting, they'll leak the video."

"I'll handle it."

34

Teddy dropped by Ben Bacchetti's office during lunch.

"Oh, hi, Mark," Ben said. Teddy, of course, was in his character-actor garb. "What can I do for you?"

"Are you still concerned with people buying up Centurion stock?"

"It's sort of in the rearview mirror. Right now my focus is on some projects to greenlight, or not. It's always a tough decision, and when it's an either/or proposition, you want to make the right choice."

"Does either/or mean you have to take one or the other?"

"No. It's more a question of do I want to commit ten million dollars to a first-time director with a fixable script, or fifteen million to a proven director with a fixable script."

"Does anyone have a script ready to go?"

"There's no such thing—most scripts require editing. Peter turns in scripts that don't need to be touched, but that's rare. Some parts of my job are simple. Greenlighting Peter is one of them."

"Uh-huh," Teddy said. "Look, I think there might be a reason to reexamine the stock situation."

"Oh? What brought that on?"

"Vanessa Morgan died. I understand she was a substantial holder."

"She was."

"What happened to the stock?"

"Her son inherited it."

"Does he have any interest in motion pictures?"

"Not that I'm aware of."

"Has that stock been transferred yet?"

"Hang on." Ben scooped up the phone. "Get me Kenny in Accounting. . . . Hi, Kenny, it's Ben. I'm wondering about Vanessa Morgan's shares of Centurion. Did they go to her son? . . . Yeah, I'll hold." Ben covered the phone. "Accountants. He knows the answer, but he's not going to tell me until he can read it off a ledger. . . . Yeah, Kenny, I'm still here. . . . Really? When did that happen? . . . Thanks, that's what I needed to know."

Ben hung up the phone. "The shares went to her son, but he turned around and sold them."

"To a holding company?"

"That's right."

"When's the next stockholders' meeting?"

"Hang on." Ben flipped open his laptop. "Let's see . . . a week from today. Damn it to hell. It seems like we just had one—I can't stand these meetings. Well, we'll get to see Peter's father, which is always a pleasure."

"These holding companies—can they vote the shares?"

"If that's what they've been instructed to do."

"This looks more and more like a hostile takeover, Ben."

"I tell you, it can't happen."

"Maybe not, but something's going on, and you don't want to be caught flatfooted. Why don't you let me attend the meeting and see if I can figure this out?"

Ben shook his head. "You're not a stockholder."

"Oh. Well, your wife's a stockholder, right? I'll go with her, as her adviser."

"She never attends. She hates stockholders' meetings, so I vote as her proxy."

"I'll talk her into it. I can be very persuasive."

"I'm not sure."

"Look, she can go because she's a stockholder. She can bring me, and give me her proxy to vote her stock. They can't kick me out if I have her proxy."

"She's not going to be happy."

"Leave it to me."

35

Tessa was amazed. "How did you swing that?"

"I'm magic," Teddy said.

"No, really."

"I convinced Ben we needed you to go in order to get me in for some reconnaissance. When he insisted you wouldn't, I told him I'd talk you into it. I'm doing that now."

"So I have to go to the meeting?"

"You *get* to go to the meeting. Before, you *had* to go to the meeting but you couldn't without raising suspicion. Now you have to go to the meeting and you *can*."

"Yes, but—"

"But what?"

"It's not enough to appear. I have to vote their way."

"You're not going to."

"Then they use the video."

"It's not going to come to that. You're going to take me with you as your adviser. If we have to vote, you're going to give me your proxy, and I'll vote your stock."

"Are you going to vote for their motion?"

"Hell, no."

"Then I'm in the same position as before. If you vote against them, it's the same as if I voted against them."

"Not exactly, and they won't be expecting it. They've invested a lot of time, energy, and money in buying up their shares—they're not going to lose their leverage and blow the deal. They'll have to regroup."

"I don't agree."

"You're scared, I understand. I'm asking you to trust me. I am not without resources. If I play my cards right, it will never come to a vote."

"How can you do that?"

"I have a plan."

Teddy felt bad saying it.

He hated to lie to friends. But he had a week to work it out.

36

Marsha Quickly slammed down the phone. Son of a bitch! What did she have an agent for, if he wasn't going to get her work? The only auditions he'd sent her for lately were cattle calls, where three hundred actresses dropped off résumés in the hope of being used in a crowd scene. None of those panned out, and anytime she scraped up anything herself, that bottom-feeding son of a bitch took fifteen percent without even lifting a finger.

Marsha was so far behind on the rent that she was dreading the day she'd get home and find the landlord had changed the lock.

Something had to give. As usual and all too common with actresses in her position, what had to give was the career.

Marsha packed everything she owned into two suitcases and snuck out, praying the super wouldn't catch her. She took a cab to the airport and blew most of her savings on a plane ticket to Las Vegas, and took a cab straight to the New Desert Inn.

Pete Genaro's curvy secretary was not welcoming. She put a

little extra sway in her step, probably for Marsha's benefit, and went in to tell the boss someone was here to see him.

Pete Genaro looked up in irritation. Everything irritated him these days, though the wiggle in Sherry's walk soothed him somewhat. "Yes," he said.

"There's a woman to see you." Sherry was not willing to favor Marsha with the adjective "young." "Says her name is Bambi."

"Who?" Genaro said.

Sherry was pleased Genaro couldn't place her. "She says she used to work here."

"Oh, I suppose she did. What does she want?"

"She wants to see you. She wasn't willing to tell her business to a secretary." Sherry smiled archly. "She brought two suitcases."

"What?"

"She brought two suitcases with her. Hard to tell if she's coming or going."

Genaro exhaled noisily. "All right. Send her in."

Marsha Quickly took one look at Genaro's face and began talking fast. "Pete, how good to see you. I didn't expect it to be so soon, but things happen. The movie business dried up, I don't know, I think it's the economy or so many TV channels, but the fact is there's no work and I can't afford to sit idle. So I'm going to be out here for a while, and of course I need a job, and who would I rather work for but you, what with our history and all."

Marsha's history with Pete Genaro consisted largely of being pinched in the ass anytime she got within arm's reach while wearing the skimpy miniskirt barmaid uniform, but Genaro wasn't listening. Sammy Candelosi was not going away, but a growing number of Genaro's employees were. Several pit bosses and dealers and barmaids had been lured over to Sammy's casino, which augured well for Marsha's chances if Pete tuned in enough to hear what she was saying.

"Don't you think?" Marsha prompted, largely to see if she had his attention. She didn't, but it snapped him out of his haze. "So if you had a position for a cocktail waitress, I know the turnover in these places is pretty rapid, and I'm someone you wouldn't have to train."

"Huh," Genaro said. The penny was starting to drop. This was someone he might need.

Marsha didn't realize she'd already made the sale. "Did you speak to Billy?" she said, reminding him of the good deed she'd done.

Genaro frowned. "Who?"

"Billy Burnett, the guy I told you about. A good man to call on if there's something you need him to take care of."

"Or someone," Genaro muttered.

"Yeah, Billy Burnett."

"What studio did you say you saw him at?"

"Centurion. Working as a stuntman."

"How about that? Billy Burnett. He changed it to Barnett, you know, when he got to Hollywood. I think I will give him a call. I have a problem he would be just the man to deal with." Genaro snatched up the phone to buzz his secretary. "In L.A., a listing for Billy Barnett." He covered the mouthpiece and nodded to Jake. "Take her down to the floor manager and tell him to put her to work. Bar girl and shill. You've worked as a shill, haven't you?"

Marsha smiled. "Are you kidding me? I was one of the best."

"Great," he replied. To Jake, "Put her to work." Into the phone he said, "Yeah, that's right. Get on the horn to him, will you?"

Teddy picked up the phone. "Hello?"

"Billy Burnett?"

"I'm afraid you have the wrong number."

"Oh, I think not. This is Pete Genaro."

"Is that supposed to mean something to me?"

"It should. I saved your life. I tipped you off that a certain Russian was on your tail. He would have killed you."

"Oh. Would that be the same Russian you hired a skip tracer for to find me so he could send his goons to kill me?"

"You don't always like your playmates. The Russian in question was an honored guest in my casino, and a member of our board of directors. When I found out what he was like, I kicked him out of my casino and had him removed from the board, and then I gave you all the information you needed to take him out."

"Why are you telling me this?"

"I find myself in a situation where I could use a little help myself. A New Jersey crime family has moved into the casino next door and is trying to crowd me out of Vegas."

"You're the toughest man in town. They can't scare you."

"These guys play dirty. The boss, Sammy Candelosi, tried to buy me out. I refused, and now he's moving in on me."

"What's he doing?"

"Making trouble for me. He killed two of his own employees so the cops would think *I* did it, as a rival. I'm totally screwed. I try to tell them what really happened, and they think I'm a lousy liar."

Teddy laughed. "You have to admire the sheer artistry of it."

"Forgive me if I fail to appreciate it. Sammy's got my employees running scared, thinking his boys are going to retaliate, and I can't calm them down because they all think I did it. My dealers and bar girls are quitting left and right to go work for him."

"It's a shame, Pete, but even if I were who you think I am, I'd be a damn fool to get involved with something like that."

"A damn fool, but a *live* damn fool. That's gotta count for something."

"Oh, come on, Pete. Didn't the thing with the Russian just come down to which one of us you'd rather see dead?"

"Don't be like that. You know I always liked you."

"Sorry. Even if I wanted to help you, I couldn't. I happen to be in a hell of a mess myself, and I don't know how I'm going to get out."

"Anything *I* could help *you* with?"

Teddy laughed. "Aw, gee, Genaro. Of all the guys that tried to kill me, I think I like you best. Listen, if I can ever help you sometime, I will, but getting involved in a mob war isn't it."

"Are you sure?"

"Sorry," Teddy said, and hung up the phone.

37

Stone Barrington flew in for the stockholders' meeting in his private Citation CJ-3 Plus. Teddy managed to tear himself away from filming to meet him at the Santa Monica airport.

Stone climbed down from the plane in front of the hangar Peter maintained for his own airplane to find Teddy standing out front.

"Who are you supposed to be?" Stone asked.

"You haven't seen my movies? I'm crushed."

"I've seen your movies, but don't get a swelled head. They also happen to be Peter's movies."

"I believe he does have something to do with them."

"You're filming this afternoon?"

"Yes, we are."

"Well, I appreciate the personal reception, but why are you here?"

Stone turned the plane over to the pilot in charge of the hangar and allowed Teddy to lead him away.

"It's about the stockholders' meeting," Teddy said.

Stone was confused. "What about it?"

"I want to go over a few things before it happens."

"Why?"

"I'm going to be there."

"You're going to attend the stockholders' meeting?"

"That's right, in the capacity of Tessa Bacchetti's adviser."

"That's not exactly your scene."

Teddy grinned. "I know. I've been an assassin for the CIA, a hit man for the mob, and a freelance killer. But I've never sunk so low as to be a corporate board member."

"What's the story?"

"Are you aware someone's been buying up Centurion stock?"

"Yes, but that's hardly surprising. It's a hot commodity."

"Well, it's being bought by several holding companies that might well be operating for the same individual. I think someone's going to attempt a hostile takeover of Centurion Pictures."

Stone started to protest.

"Yes, I know," Teddy said. "You control over fifty percent of the stock. But the way I understand it, the girls have fifteen percent between them."

Stone's face darkened. "If you're dragging the kids into this . . . "

"Not at all," Teddy said. "You know me better than that. I'm taking precautions in case someone else tries to drag the kids into this. I'll be at the meeting. I'm going with Tessa Bacchetti just to get in the door. She normally gives Ben her proxy to vote her stock. This time she'll be there in person with me as her adviser and give *me* her proxy so they can't throw me out."

"What aren't you telling me?"

"The more you know, the more you feel you have to act. I owe you big time for the presidential pardon."

"You've more than paid that back."

"I can never pay that back. I'm happy to help in small ways."

"If you want to pay me back, tell me what's happening."

Teddy smiled. "Nice try, Stone."

38

Stone took everyone out to dinner, bypassing the more trendy Hollywood restaurants in favor of an old-fashioned steakhouse that'd been around for more than fifty years. Sylvia Kenmore, the well-known film star Peter Barrington had invited as a date for his father, was no vegetarian, and he knew the others in his party would approve. They included Peter and Hattie Barrington, Ben and Tessa Bacchetti, and Teddy Fay, on hand as producer Billy Barnett.

Peter and Hattie would have been happy to host the dinner at their place, but Stone wanted to relieve everyone of any responsibility while he was there. "After all," he told Peter, "you're making a movie."

After they had ordered and their drinks had arrived, Stone raised a glass. "To the movies. May people never stop going."

"What? Did you hear something?" Sylvia said, and everybody laughed.

"It's a problem already, I fear," Stone said. "All these streaming services allow people to view movies cheaply, from the comfort of their own homes. Without box office takes, the financing for future films becomes tricky."

"I don't think we'll ever see the end of big cinema," Teddy said, "because the movies still deliver something that streaming can't. Nothing beats the experience of being in the theater when everyone laughs at something funny or gasps in suspense. As long as you move an audience, you'll get an audience."

An actor walked by. "Isn't that Leonardo DiCaprio?" Sylvia said.

"I have no idea," Tessa said. "So many of these actors have beards these days I can't tell anyone apart."

"If it is Leonardo DiCaprio," Peter said, "I bet he's over there saying, isn't that Sylvia Kenmore?"

"How's the picture coming?" Stone said.

"Good," Peter said.

"Better than good," Ben said. "I've seen the dailies. I think it's Peter's best work yet." He put his arm around Tessa. "I'm not just saying that because my wife is fantastic."

"Isn't Brad Hunter kind of a stiff?" Stone said.

"We need the name to get the wider distribution, and Peter has drawn an amazing performance out of him."

"It's our stunt man who's kind of a stiff," Peter said, grinning.

"Yeah, but he works for scale," Teddy said, and everybody laughed.

Sylvia looked around, puzzled. "Is that an inside joke?"

"It's a bit of an inside joke," Stone said. "He's a friend of ours."

Peter turned to Sylvia. "I wanted to ask you to read for my next film."

"I'd be delighted," she said.

"As would we," Ben said. "You'd be perfect for the part."

There was a break in the conversation while the entrées were served. As they dug in, Peter said, "Oh, I didn't tell you. Tessa's mother's sick."

"Really?" Stone said. He felt a personal connection, having dated her.

Tessa blushed furiously. "It's nothing really. Just a scare. She thought it was something, but it wasn't. The tests were all negative."

"What was it?" Stone said. He was genuinely concerned.

"You never mentioned she was having tests," Ben said, confused and alarmed. He put his hand over Tessa's.

"She's been quite private about it, and I know she didn't want it widely known. And in any case, it amounted to nothing. I never should have mentioned it in the first place."

"Oh, I know those scares," Sylvia Kenmore said.

The rest of the meal went smoothly.

Teddy managed to sidle up to Tessa on the way out. "Remind me to teach you about lying," he whispered.

Tessa ignored him and kept walking.

"It's called Telling Stories That Don't Come Back to Bite You 101."

39

The stockholders' meeting was held in the boardroom at Centurion Studios, and was scheduled during the lunch break so Peter could attend. Present were Stone Barrington, Peter Barrington, Ben Bacchetti, Tessa Tweed Bacchetti and her adviser, and a bespectacled young man in a business suit. Peter had given Mark Weldon a day off from filming so Teddy could come as Billy Barnett.

"Very well," Stone said, calling the meeting to order. "I regret we have only the lunch break, but Centurion is in the business of making motion pictures. I know everyone here but you, sir. And who might you be?"

"Todd Reynolds. I'm here representing Glendale Management, Venn Holding, Everest Holding, and the USB Corporation."

"All four?" Stone said. "You don't find that a conflict of interest?"

"No, I do not. This is my first meeting, and I don't really know anyone."

"I beg your pardon. I'm Stone Barrington. This is Ben Bacchetti, Peter Barrington, Tessa Tweed Bacchetti, and Billy Barnett."

Todd Reynolds had his briefcase open on the table and was consulting a file folder in his lap. "I see. I have a list of stockholders here. I do not find the name Barnett."

"Mr. Barnett is here with Mrs. Bacchetti as her adviser. This is her first meeting and she wanted support."

The young man made a *tsk-tsk* sound. "My clients would object to the presence of anyone not holding stock."

"And just who are your clients?"

"The four holding companies I mentioned."

"And whom do they represent?"

"Oh, I couldn't divulge the identity of their clients without permission."

Stone nodded. "Get it."

"I beg your pardon?"

"I suggest you get their permission."

Todd Reynolds frowned. "The confidentiality of my clients is not the issue. We're getting off the subject. If this gentleman is not a stockholder, he has no right to be here."

"Mrs. Bacchetti has given me her proxy so I can vote her stock," Teddy said.

The young man's mask slipped momentarily. His smile became a scowl. "She can't do that."

"Of course she can," Stone said. "Anyone can. In fact, she has always given her proxy ever since she's been a stockholder. She can give her proxy to anyone she chooses. Now, I don't mean to be rude, but I've come all the way from New York for this meeting, and we only have the lunch hour to hold it. So if we could not get bogged down on parliamentary procedure, I'd like to get down to the business at hand. As I understand it, you have a matter you wish to address."

Todd Reynolds took a breath. "Yes, I do." He reached in his briefcase and took out stapled packets of paper. He slid them around the table in front of the stockholders. "The people I represent have compiled a cost-benefit analysis of Centurion Pictures. While it shows a profit, it is a small profit, and dependent on a fluctuating economy. They therefore propose that they take the helm of Centurion Pictures and guide it to the profitable business they are sure it can be. I hereby move that Ben Bacchetti be ousted as the head of production of Centurion Pictures and Glendale Management be installed in his place."

"What!" Tessa cried.

"That's outrageous!" Peter cried. "How dare you!"

"Are you serious?" Ben cried.

Only Teddy sat silent.

When the noise had died down, Todd Reynolds said, "I hereby make that motion. Do I hear a second?" He looked straight at Tessa Tweed.

Tessa looked at Teddy.

"You sure as hell do not!" Peter snapped.

"How about it, Mrs. Bacchetti? Just because the man is your husband does not make you any less responsible to the stockholders. Do I hear a second?"

"Well, now, you should be addressing me," Teddy said, "since I hold her proxy. I must say this is a very interesting idea, and just because all the individuals involved know each other is no reason to reject it out of hand. It's important not to rush to judgment. I therefore move we adjourn until we have had time to study your proposal."

"You can't do that. I already have a motion on the floor."

"Actually," Teddy said, "you attempted to get a motion on the floor, but it wasn't seconded. The motion to adjourn is always in order. I so move."

"Second," Peter said.

"It's been moved and seconded that we adjourn until we have time to study your proposal. I have to go back to New York, but I can be here in"—Stone consulted the calendar on his phone—"two weeks. Let's adjourn until two weeks from today. It's been moved and seconded that we adjourn. All in favor."

"Aye."

"All opposed."

"Nay," Todd Reynolds said.

"The ayes have it. The meeting is adjourned."

40

Teddy, Tessa, and Ben made their way to the parking lot, Ben still fuming and incredulous.

"What the hell is going on?" Ben Bacchetti wanted to know.

"It's a hostile takeover, just like I thought."

"I know that," Ben said. "I mean, what were you doing in there?"

"I bought us two weeks."

"We don't need two weeks—we can take care of the problem now. The guy brought a motion, you could have just voted it down."

"Then we won't know what's going on, or who's behind all of this. I want to find out who they are and deal with them so it doesn't happen again."

"Yes, but as long as we can vote them down . . ."

"They're a pain in the ass," Teddy said. "They don't have a controlling interest, but they are the largest single stockholder."

"But they're not a single stockholder," Ben said. "This guy represents four separate holding companies."

"And we don't know who their client is," Teddy said. "I'm going to find out."

The young man with the briefcase came out and walked across the lot.

"There's Todd Reynolds now," Teddy said. "Go back inside as if this was all a matter of course, and we were just talking business as usual."

Teddy turned his back on Tessa and Ben and walked across the lot to his car. He hopped in, pulled out of the space reserved for Billy Barnett, and drove past Todd Reynolds, who was walking toward the main gate. Either his car was parked outside the lot or he had come by cab.

Todd Reynolds walked to a small sedan, got in, and drove off. Teddy followed cautiously. The young man didn't appear to have a clue he was being tailed, but Teddy hadn't survived this long by taking things for granted.

Todd Reynolds drove downtown and pulled into a lot next to an office building. It was a small lot, and there was no way Teddy could pull in behind him without being spotted.

There was a cop on the corner. Teddy stopped next to him, slapped a Centurion Pictures placard on the dashboard, hopped out, and said, "Watch my car."

Sometimes it worked. If it didn't, he'd get a ticket, a towing charge, and a hefty fine, but that was a fair trade-off.

Todd Reynolds had already gone into the building. Teddy hurried to the front door, and through the glass saw Todd

Reynolds waiting for the elevator. Unfortunately, so were three other people, so Teddy wouldn't be able to tell which floor he got off on by watching the indicator.

Teddy whipped out his wallet and opened the door just as the elevator door closed on Todd Reynolds.

Teddy ran up to the front desk. "The young man with the briefcase who just got on the elevator. Where is he going?"

The man at the desk shook his head.

"I know," Teddy said, "you don't give out that information. The guy just dropped his wallet." He held it up. "I tried to catch him, but I'm not as fast as I used to be."

"You can give it to me. I'll see that he gets it."

"I think not," Teddy said. "I want to give it to him personally, with the money in it so he can see that it's all there. I'm sure he'll be grateful."

"You think he'll give you a tip," the guard said.

"And you think he'll give you one. But you didn't run two blocks with the damn thing. Come on. You have the register there. Look the guy up and tell me where he works."

"Let's see the wallet."

Teddy smiled. "I'm holding on to it." He flipped it open, pretending to read the ID. "His name is Todd Reynolds."

The receptionist at Glendale Management was holding a telephone to her ear. As Teddy approached the desk she said, "Hold, please, for Mr. Dirkson." She pressed another line and said, "Mr. Dirkson? Mr. Williams on three." She looked up and smiled at Teddy. "May I help you?"

"Todd Reynolds, please."

"I'm sorry, he's not in his office."

"Oh? That's odd. I'm supposed to have a meeting with him. If you could ring his cell phone."

She shook her head. "I can't disturb him. He's in with Mr. Dirkson."

"Perfect. I'm supposed to meet with him, too. It's this way?" Teddy was already around the desk and making his way to the door marked DIRECTOR.

The receptionist sprang up. "You can't go in there."

"Actually, I can," Teddy said, and pushed the door open.

Todd Reynolds stood talking to a plump man with three chins who was sitting behind a large desk.

"Ah, Mr. Dirkson, I presume. Just the man I wanted to see. Todd said you were the man I wanted to talk to."

The fat man looked at his subordinate. "Todd?"

"I did no such thing," Todd sputtered. "This is the man from the meeting. He must have followed me here."

"You let yourself be followed?" Dirkson said.

Teddy flopped into a chair, pulled a humidor of cigars across the desk, and inspected one. "Don't blame him. He's an amateur." He pointed the cigar at the fat man. "You're the one to blame, promising your lowlife clients anonymity."

"Get out of here or I'll call the police."

"Good idea. They'll get some answers. They'll certainly want to know on whose behalf you're having me arrested. Do you think you can stand up to a police investigation?"

Dirkson snatched up the phone. "Margo, get me the police."

Teddy nodded approvingly. "Nicely played. Most men

would fold in your position. It's plain to see you're a pro. Excellent. I was trying to ascertain how complicit you are in the situation. It's clear you're a main participant."

"Now, see here—"

"No, no," Teddy said, waggling his finger. "You can't throw me out and give me a lecture. Pick one."

The phone rang. Dirkson scooped it up. His eyes never left Teddy. "Yes? . . . No, not now." He slammed the phone down again. "Are you going to leave of your own accord?"

"Absolutely," Teddy said. He rose from the chair. "I'm sorry you don't feel inclined to discuss this amicably. Mr. Reynolds made quite an interesting motion at today's meeting. I was hoping to learn more about it."

Dirkson didn't bite. He just sat there and waited until Teddy left.

Teddy stopped on his way out and smiled at the receptionist. "Did you get through to the police?"

She frowned. "I thought the call was canceled."

"It's all right, I'll call them myself."

Teddy whipped out his cell phone and began punching in numbers.

The telephone buzzed. The receptionist picked it up and said, "Yes, sir." She clicked on a line and punched in a number. "Mr. Dirkson for Mr. Kimble. One moment, please." She picked up the first line. "Mr. Kimble on two."

Teddy looked up from his cell phone. "Busy," he said. He shook his head, shrugged, and rang for the elevator.

41

Teddy stopped by the Centurion office.

Ben jumped up when he came in. "What happened? Did you find out who he represents?"

"Not yet, but I'm working on it. Do know anyone in the industry named Kimble?"

"Why? Is that him?"

"I'm not sure. Do you know him?"

"I don't know him, but there's a B-movie producer named Mason Kimble. I'd hardly flatter him by saying he's in the industry. He has his own company, Star Pictures, and he makes the kind of movies you wouldn't let your kids go to. Low-budget shoot-'em-ups with a lot of gratuitous violence and nudity, and not much plot."

"Does he have any reason not to like you?"

"Why?"

"These guys are trying to oust you as the head of production. Either it's business or it's personal. If this Mason Kimble is behind it, would he have any reason to hate you?"

Ben shrugged. "He pitched a project to me and I shot it down, but that's hardly grounds. He couldn't possibly have thought I would seriously consider his film. I figured he pitched it to me so he could tell people he did."

"Some people have an unrealistic assessment of their own worth. Okay, he's one possibility. Is there anyone else you've shot down who might have reason to take it personally? Anyone who might regard it as a slight?"

"I've rejected a number of projects. Most producers take it as a matter of course. I suppose there are screenwriters who might feel their work had been unfairly assessed."

"Any screenwriter who might be successful enough to buy up nearly half the Centurion stock?"

"I suppose it's possible."

Teddy considered. "Do you have a slush pile of rejected scripts?"

"Are you looking for one of Mason Kimble's?"

"No, but I'm glad you mentioned it. Can I see them?"

"In the outer office. Janet can show you. You don't have to read them, we keep the coverage."

Centurion, like many movie studios, hired interns to write two-page summaries and assessments of screenplays for producers to use as shorthand.

"Thanks," Teddy said. "That will help."

Janet set Teddy at a table with a pile of scripts to look at. He sorted through them, careful to choose one that was not associated with Mason Kimble. The coverage was most helpful in narrowing down the type of script he had in mind. He chose one entitled *Night Noises*. The reader's report described it as "an erotic thriller" with "more nudity than scares."

Teddy turned back to the title page:

NIGHT NOISES by Rick Grogan.

Teddy crossed out Rick Grogan and penciled in Cy Henderson. He handed the screenplay to Janet.

"Type me a new title page, will you?"

42

want to make a movie," Teddy said. He said it with the exaggerated emphasis of an old man who expects to get his way. For his meeting with Mason Kimble, Teddy had made himself up as a wealthy eccentric, with wild hair and tie carelessly askew.

Teddy slapped a screenplay down on Mason's desk. "*Night Noises*. Great title. A lot of meanings, all of them good."

Mason glanced at Gerard Cardigan, who sat off to the side. "Did you write this, Mr. Jackson?"

"Hell, no. I bought it. I read it, I said I want to make this movie. My question is whether you want to make it, too."

"It takes a lot of money to make a motion picture."

"How much?"

"This is not some fly-by-night production. You're talking about a major motion picture."

"How much?"

"Five million dollars," Mason said. He was careful not to

look at Gerard Cardigan. To date, their biggest budget had been half a million.

Teddy frowned. "That's more than I invested last time. Quite a bit more. I'm not saying it's not doable."

"Was your last production successful?"

"My last movie was a pain in the ass. I put up the money, and they didn't want me on the set, said I made this actress nervous. I'm paying her fucking salary—what right has she got to be nervous? That's the first thing right up front. There's girls in this picture. Cute girls. And I wanna be there when you film them."

"Is there nudity in the script?"

"What's that got to do with anything? The cameraman's there, you're there, the soundman's there. Are they wearing blindfolds? You got an actress doesn't want to do it, don't hire 'em. You got a clause right in the contract, don't you?" Teddy pointed to the movie posters of Star Pictures productions, many of which featured scantily clad young ladies. "I suppose none of these pictures have nudity."

Mason took that as his cue to brag about his own work.

Teddy tuned out and sized up the young men. Mason Kimble was pretty much what he expected—an arrogant young blowhard pumping himself up by pretending to be something he could never be.

Gerard Cardigan was the wild card. Teddy hadn't expected Gerard, but meeting him cleared some things up. Mason was a lightweight, but Gerard was dangerous. There was something cold and calculating in his look that gave Teddy a chill. He had seen that same look in the eyes of a serial killer once, just before he shot him dead. The young man was proof, had Teddy needed any, that Vanessa Morgan drowning in her bathtub had not been an accident.

Teddy was particularly interested in the young men, and had been ever since he walked into their studio. A DVD player was connected to the TV in front of the desk.

Teddy asked a few more bullshit questions, familiarized himself with the layout of the office, and got the hell out.

W hat do you think?" Mason asked Gerard, after Teddy left. "I think we're in the middle of something big. Why do you want to jeopardize it for five million? Do you really believe this guy's going to come up with that kind of money? I couldn't believe it when I heard you say it."

"I said five million to scare him off. He didn't scare."

"Exactly," Gerard said.

"What do you mean by that?"

"Nothing. Maybe. But do me a favor, just forget about him."

"Why?"

"This is a guy you normally wouldn't waste your time with, but you are. I'll tell you why. The takeover bid failed. You had a big letdown, and you need a big rush to make yourself feel better. Well, that guy isn't it. I know it, and you know it, so forget about him and get back to the task at hand. The girl fucked with us, and we need to take action."

"Send her a cell phone."

"How?"

"Leave it in her trailer and watch to see when she gets it. It scares her when she picks it up and it rings."

"Fine," Gerard said. He got a burner cell phone from the cabinet and slipped it into a mailer. "And do me a favor, will you?"

"What?"

"Take the DVD out of the safe and lock it up at home."

"Why?"

"Just a feeling."

43

Teddy broke into Star Pictures at two in the morning. He didn't expect security to be much, and it wasn't. He was through the downstairs door in minutes. The upstairs hall boasted a camera aimed at the ceiling. Teddy ignored it and picked the lock on the door.

Working with a small flashlight, Teddy made his way around the office, peering behind every hanging movie poster until he found what he was looking for—a concealed safe. He was out of practice. It took him nearly ten minutes to open.

Teddy found a couple of contracts and some money, but no DVD.

Teddy searched the desk and found nothing of interest.

Not to ignore the obvious, he popped the tray on the DVD player. It was empty.

Fifteen minutes later Teddy left the office empty-handed.

Either the DVD had never been there or somehow he had tipped his hand.

Teddy went home to get some sleep. Things would be hopping in the morning. Not only did he have to be on the set, but he expected they would start feeling the repercussions of the stockholders' meeting.

44

Tessa wasn't surprised to find another mailer containing a new cell phone. After the board meeting, she expected it. Once again, it rang as soon as she found it in her trailer, indicating that someone was watching her. She hadn't noticed anyone outside, and she had been looking.

"Hello?"

"You've been a bad girl, Tessa."

"I have not."

"And now you're talking back. That's a very bad girl."

"I've done everything you asked."

"Now, you know that isn't true."

"I went to the meeting."

"You brought someone."

"I had to. I've never been to a stockholders' meeting. I didn't know what to do."

"I told you what to do."

"You told me how to vote. You didn't tell me how to conduct myself in a meeting. It's complicated."

"And now you're making up excuses. You must want to be a viral star."

"You know I don't or I wouldn't be cooperating."

"Cooperating? I am very unhappy with this man you brought to the meeting."

"He's a producer who knows the ropes."

"He knows how to stall. I don't like being stalled. He won't be at the next meeting."

"Won't people think it strange if he isn't?"

"Do you really think I care?"

"You want the meeting to go smoothly."

"You really like to argue, don't you? That could be one of the captions with your pictures, like they used to have with the girls in *Playboy*. 'Likes to water paint in her spare time.' Mr. Barnett will not be at the next meeting. Just you, nobody else."

"How can I keep him from going?"

He chuckled. "You won't have a problem in that respect."

"Why not?"

"You just won't."

Tessa pulled Teddy off the set. "He called again."

"Was he angry?"

"Oh, yes."

"Did he make threats?"

"Against you."

"How did he threaten me?"

"He said you won't be at the next meeting. I asked how I'd stop you from coming, and he said that won't be a problem."

"That's a rather oblique threat."

"Yes, but it's a threat."

"And that's good."

"How is that good?"

"He's threatening me and not you, and he didn't post the video."

"He threatened to."

"Of course he did, but he can't follow through or he loses his leverage. I bought us two weeks. He doesn't like it, but there's nothing he can do about it."

"He implied he's going to kill you."

"Aw, well, he's not the first person to have said so."

"You're not worried?"

"I'm worried, but I'm worried about a lot of things. An unidentified voice on the phone implying that he'd like to kill me is not at the top of the list. Anyway, the guy called you up to piss and moan. That's good, it means that's all he can do right now. I doubt if he'll be calling back. He's more or less forced to wait for the next meeting to take place. There's not much he can do until then."

"I hope you're right," Tessa said.

She didn't sound convinced.

45

Pete Genaro sent Jake to check up on Sammy Candelosi. Two more of Genaro's employees had defected, and he wanted to find out what type of coercion Sammy was using.

Genaro didn't know it, but Jake had gone over, too. When Pete sent him to see how Sammy was handling the death of his two employees, Slythe had held a straight razor to his throat, and Sammy had offered him the choice of becoming a counter-spy or a corpse. Jake had opted to remain among the living, and had been spying on both men ever since.

So far Genaro hadn't noticed that everything Jake told him was something he already knew.

Sammy Candelosi was not so gullible. "You're giving me shit. You're giving me things I already know. What you're giv-ing me as intel is absolutely worthless. It makes me think you're still working for Genaro. That's the trouble with this double-agent shit—you can play either side. Well, I don't intend to be played. If you don't give me something I can use, then I will believe you're working for him, and if you're working for him, you are a *large* liability. You are something that I cannot afford to deal with. I would be forced to cut my losses. And my loss is not going to be Genaro's gain, if you know what I mean."

Sammy cocked his head in his henchman's direction. "I'm sure Slythe knows what I mean."

Slythe's expression never changed, but his reptilian eyes seemed to be sizing Jake up.

Jake swallowed hard. "I've told you everything I know. It's not that I'm holding back. It's that you got his number. He doesn't know how to handle you, or, believe me, he would."

"I'm not surprised he doesn't tell you things, but you must hear shit. Aren't you ever in his office when something's going on? Or are you telling me nothing's going on? If you tell me nothing's going on and something's going on, you are going to be the sorriest individual who ever lived."

Jake gasped. "Oh, shit!"

"I had a feeling this conversation would jog your memory."

"An out-of-town hitter." Jake nodded in agreement with himself. "Pete hired a bar girl to replace one of the ones he lost to you, and she suggested this out-of-town hitter. Christ, what was the name?"

"You better have the fucking name."

"I wasn't there when he made the call. It's a guy in L.A., works in the movies."

"Works in the movies?" Sammy said skeptically.

"He works in the movies now. He didn't always. He used to be here in Vegas, and made trouble for Pete."

"Then why would Pete want him?"

"It's complicated. But the bar girl suggested it and he said maybe he'd give him a call."

"Who?" Sammy said. The edge in his voice was frightening.

Out of the corner of his eye, Jake could see Slythe pull out his razor.

"Wait! Wait!" Jake cried. He was thinking hard. "It was just before I took the girl out to meet the floor manager. And Pete picked up the phone and asked his secretary to find an L.A. listing for a . . . Billy Burnett! That's it! Billy Burnett!" Jake frowned. "Only that wasn't right."

"What?" Sammy said ominously.

"No. That's what Pete said. He said it wasn't Burnett any-more, the guy changed it to *Barnett*. It was Billy Barnett. A pro-ducer in Hollywood."

"He asked for the listing of Billy Barnett?"

"That's right. The secretary was going to try to find his num-ber, and that's when I left."

"And you didn't think this was important enough to tell me about?"

"Nothing came of it. He never mentioned it again."

"Did he get the guy on the phone?"

"I don't know. He never said."

"And you couldn't ask?"

"Pete's sharp. If I start pumping him for information about his dealings, he'll be suspicious and I'll be in trouble."

"More trouble than you're in now?"

Jake said nothing, hoped it was over.

It wasn't.

"This guy is supposedly good?" Sammy said.

"To hear Pete tell it, he was one of the best."

Sammy nodded imperceptibly. Slythe slipped the straight razor back into his pocket. "Okay, good to know. Keep your ears open. If you find out anything, anything at all, about Billy Barnett—without blowing your cover," Sammy conceded in a mockingly ironic tone, "you bring it straight to me."

S lythe watched Jake go out. "When are you going to let me kill him?"

"When he stops being useful."

"How will you know?"

Sammy chuckled. "Patience," he said. He frowned thoughtfully. "I'm concerned about this Billy Barnett."

"You want to know what he's doing?" Slythe said.

"I don't care what he's doing," Sammy said. "I just don't want him to do it."

Slythe's face relaxed. Without changing expression, he resembled a contented cat. "Then he won't."

46

S lythe flew into L.A. He waited impatiently at baggage claim. He had no clothes, but there was no way his straight razor would make it through security. He collected the small bag he had checked for that purpose, rented a car, and drove into town. He stopped at the first closed gas station he came to and put a rock through the window. He went in and stole every gas can he could find. It took him two more gas stations to get as many cans as he needed.

He drove to an open self-service station and managed to fill the cans while pretending to fill his tank.

He stopped at a news kiosk, bought a couple of newspapers, and drove out to Billy Barnett's address.

The Barnett residence was a two-story house set back from the street. The lights were on, and there was a car in the drive.

Slythe drove by slowly. As he passed the house, he could see someone in the living room. He checked the time. Ten-fifteen. Good. Billy Barnett shouldn't be up long. He was a movie person, and movie people had early calls. A producer would want to be on the set, parading around like a big shot and impressing the actresses.

Slythe began driving irregular patterns through the neighborhood, occasionally passing Billy Barnett's house in different directions at varying speeds.

By eleven-twenty the light was out and the car was still there.

Perfect.

Slythe found an all-night diner and ordered French toast. He sat sipping coffee and reading the papers he had bought. Around one-thirty he availed himself of the bathroom, paid his bill, and took one last swing around Billy Barnett's neighborhood. By now all the homes were dark.

He parked two houses down and began the laborious task of lugging the gas cans to the house.

47

Teddy woke up and smelled smoke. He was sleeping upstairs, which saved his life. By the time he leaped out of bed, the downstairs was a blazing inferno. He grabbed his gun off the nightstand. If the fire was due to natural causes, he wouldn't need it, but if it had been set on purpose to drive him out in the open, he'd be a sitting duck.

Teddy touched the doorknob and found it warm but not hot. When he opened the bedroom door, the hallway was ablaze, the stairs were blocked, and flames were licking up from below. Teddy slammed shut the door and rushed to the window. It was worse. The window was engulfed and already too hot to get near.

Teddy backed into the center of the room, thinking hard. He ran back to the door. The knob was heating up, but still cool enough to turn. He wrenched it open again. There was no way to get to the stairs, but at the other end of the hall there was a spare bedroom he never used. There was no furniture in it to burn, and the floor was covered with linoleum, which might be flame retardant. It was a long shot, but a long shot was all he had.

Teddy held his breath to avoid the smoke and sprinted down the fiery hallway. He wrenched the spare bedroom door open and plunged in.

The linoleum appeared to be fireproof, but it was peeling up from the floor, and the boards beneath it were glowing embers.

The window was engulfed in flames, but he had to get to it. He darted gingerly across the room, careful to step on what linoleum still clung to the floor. He tried for the window, but it was already too hot to touch. He took a step back into the middle of the room and glanced around desperately for another way to escape.

Teddy heaved a huge sigh, breathing in what was now largely carbon dioxide, in helpless frustration.

There was no way out.

Slythe approached through the bushes. There was no danger of being discovered. He would hear the sirens long before the police and firemen arrived on the scene.

It would be fast. He had taken pains to ensure it would be fast, drenching the house in gasoline on all four sides, and pouring gas through the windows to make sure the interior went up as fast. He just had to see with his own eyes that no one got out. No one could get out. Even so, it was important to know for sure.

The house was ablaze, and it had taken only seconds. Billy

Barnett could not even have gotten up that fast. Most likely he would be overcome with heat and smoke and die in his bed. Every second that passed made escape less and less possible.

Slythe worked his way around the house, making sure that each and every direction was blocked. It was. The flames had enveloped the upstairs windows and reached the roof. Still, should a hopelessly charred figure stumble blindly from the house, his razor was ready for the coup de grâce.

The first siren was heard in the distance, followed immediately by another. That was it. It was over. They were coming.

Slythe headed back to the car.

An upstairs window shattered. A shapeless form hurtled through it and landed on the lawn.

Slythe started for it.

The shapeless form was a man. He shrugged off the linoleum he'd been wrapped in and stood up.

Slythe froze. His mouth fell open.

He had a gun?

It wasn't enough that he was alive and apparently unharmed. He was holding a gun!

There was no way Slythe could take him on with just a straight razor. Not someone as good as this guy apparently was.

Slythe backed into the shadows.

The sirens were louder.

Slythe crept around the house and headed for his car. He drove off just as the first fire trucks and police cars pulled up.

48

Teddy's property was surrounded by four fire trucks, six police cars, and two ambulances. For all that, they hadn't managed to save his house. By the time he had woken up it was pretty much gone.

A policeman was talking to Teddy on the front lawn. "You woke up and smelled smoke?"

Teddy figured the cop suspected him of arson. The house was totaled, and he had barely a scratch. "That's right."

Teddy was still dressed in his pajamas. He had managed to stash the gun in his glove compartment before the cops arrived, or the conversation would have taken a whole different turn.

A cop hurried up to them. Teddy couldn't help thinking he was so young he must be thrilled to be up past his bedtime.

"It's arson all right. There are gas cans scattered all around the place."

"Did you collect them for fingerprints?"

"It's being done."

"Without fucking them up?"

"I'm on it," the cop said, and hurried away.

"This is your house?"

"That's right."

"And your name is?"

"Billy Barnett."

"Can I see your identification?"

Teddy jerked his thumb in the direction of the fire. "It's in there. Look, I'm the owner, so I know you need to check whether or not I burned it down for the insurance money. It's insured for the bare minimum, and I never increased it. If you asked me if I'd rather have the money or the house, I'd take the house, because I guarantee you I won't be able to buy anything as good with what I'll get as a payout."

An EMS worker from one of the ambulances came over. "Sir, you're going to the hospital?"

"No, I'm fine."

"We still need to check you out."

"Go ahead."

"You mind sitting on the back of the ambulance? We want to check your blood pressure."

"Officer," Teddy said, "may I suggest a change of venue? I'd like to get these guys squared away."

They walked over to the ambulance. Teddy sat down, and they strapped on the blood pressure cuff.

"One-thirty over seventy," the EMS worker said.

"A little high from the excitement," Teddy said.

The EMS guy said, "High?"

Teddy checked out fine. He had a few cuts and scratches

from the broken window, but they were superficial. His forearms had taken the brunt of it. The medic cleaned them up, dabbed on antibiotic, and pronounced him good to go.

"How about it, Officer?" Teddy said. "What do you say you check with Motor Vehicles, pull up my driver's license, verify I am who I say I am, and let me get a room for the night? We're shooting first thing in the morning, and it's going to be hard getting up."

"You're in the movie business?"

"Yes."

"Who do you work for?"

"Centurion."

"What do you do there?"

"I'm a producer."

The Hollywood community was divided between people who were impressed with a producer and those who considered him nonessential personnel. The cop clearly fell in the latter category.

Still, he ran Teddy's driver's license and let him go. Teddy knew he would. He had been Billy Barnett long enough that his cover was damn near perfect.

49

Teddy drove up to the Arrington Hotel, handed his car off to the valet service, and walked into the lobby in his pajamas with his gun in a paper bag.

The woman behind the desk was surprised to see him, to say the least. She gulped and said, "Sir?"

"I'm Billy Barnett. I'm going to be staying at Stone Barrington's house. It's spur of the moment, and I don't have a key. I understand Stone keeps a key at the desk for emergencies."

"Sir?"

"I apologize for my appearance. My house burned down. If you check with the police, you will find it just happened."

"That's not the issue. In the absence of Stone Barrington, I would have to clear this with Peter Barrington. And he can't be reached at this hour."

Teddy held out his hand. "Give me the phone."

She frowned.

"Mine burned up. I need your phone."

Teddy called and got Peter's answering service. The service

was an improvement over voice mail, because Peter was able to leave specific messages for specific callers.

The woman on the line was clearly used to fielding calls at all hours. "Peter Barrington's line."

"This is Billy Barnett. Put me through to Peter Barrington."

"I'm sorry, Mr. Barnett. Mr. Barrington does not accept calls at this hour."

"He'll accept mine."

"I have no instructions to that effect."

"What are your instructions?"

"Not to ring him for anything short of a fire."

"Then you won't get in trouble. My house just burned down, which is going to affect tomorrow's shooting unless I speak to him now."

A minute later Peter's groggy voice came on the line. "This better be good."

"It's not. I'm at the Arrington. My house burned down."

"What?"

"Yeah. You attend one little stockholders' meeting, and—"

"Billy."

"Relax. I'm sure it has nothing to do with that. But the fact is, my house burned down, along with everything in it. I've got the pajamas I was wearing, and that's it. So if you expect Mark Weldon to show up on the set tomorrow, I'm going to need some clean clothes and a makeup kit sent over to Stone's house. I figure if anyone can make that happen this time of night, it's the director. You also need to vouch for me with the Arrington desk clerk. She seems pretty freaked out."

"Oh my God," Peter said.

50

Peter Barrington came through. At five o'clock in the morning a fully equipped makeup kit and a complete change of inconspicuous clothing were delivered to Stone Barrington's residence adjacent to the Arrington Hotel. Per Peter's instructions, the production assistant entrusted with the task did not ring the doorbell, but merely left the items on the stoop. The gofer was getting a generous tip for the service, and an even larger tip not to talk about it. There was nothing odd in that. What movie folk did was nobody's business.

As soon as the young man was gone, Teddy inspected the items. His main concern was the makeup kit. It wasn't nearly as good as his own, but it would do, at least to get stuntman Mark Weldon onto the back lot and into wardrobe and makeup, where a wig and costume would transform him into movie villain Leonard Kirk.

Teddy had gotten to the studio and just finished changing when Tessa walked onto the set. She was shocked. "Your house burned down?"

Teddy grabbed her arm and pulled her away. "No, no, no, you must be confused. *Billy Barnett*'s house burned down," he said meaningfully.

Her eyes widened. "Of course, *Mark*, how silly of me."

"It happens to the best of us."

"And where is Mark Weldon's house, exactly?"

"That's something I'm going to have to take care of. It never was an issue before now. Nobody on this picture needed to know my address, so I didn't need to have one."

"Damn it," Tessa said. "I don't care what you're going to tell everybody else. What happened?"

"My house burned down. It was arson. Someone tried to kill me in my bed."

"Oh my God!"

"Relax, I'm fine. But someone burned my house. They did a thorough job of it, too, completely drenched it with gasoline. It was pretty extensive for arson, more likely enough to ensure nobody got out."

"Was it because of me?"

"Don't get a swelled head. Just because you're a movie star, the world doesn't revolve around you."

"Billy, I'm not in the mood."

"Mark, I'm not in the mood," Teddy corrected. "The more you do it when we're alone, the more chance you'll do it in front of someone else."

"Is this because of the meeting?"

"It could be," Teddy said. As far as he was concerned, it was equally likely it was because of things he had done after the meeting, but there was no reason to tell her about that.

"Is it about the gun?"

"Interesting idea. I'll have to think about that."

"Where is it?"

"I'm glad you asked."

Tessa waited. "Well?"

"Oh, I'm not going to tell you. But thanks for reminding me. I've got a lot of things to remember."

"Did it burn up in the fire?"

"Another interesting idea. I'm afraid guns don't burn very well."

"Then—"

"Tessa, I'm handling it. You just worry about things you've got to worry about."

"I'm not that type of girl."

Teddy sighed. "No, you're not. That's what I like about you, but it's damn exhausting."

"Aren't you worried?"

"Worried about what?"

"That someone tried to kill you."

"Well, he didn't succeed."

"You're taking it so casually."

"When something like this happens, you have to keep a clear head and assess the situation. What happens, happens."

"What happened was someone burned down your house."

Teddy shrugged. "There *are* glitches."

51

Mason Kimble looked up from the newspaper. "Did you burn his house down?"

"Who?" Gerard said.

"Billy Barnett."

"No. Do you want me to burn his house down?"

"Someone already did."

"What?"

"His house burned down last night. He barely escaped with his life. Are you sure you didn't do that?" Gerard had been known to use forceful methods to deal with problems.

"Barnett escaped. Does that sound like my work?"

"No offense meant, but what the hell is going on?"

Gerard shrugged. "All of this is news to me. I don't know anything about this Billy Barnett person, except he's chosen to make himself a major pain in the ass. The last I heard, we have two weeks to deal with him. But rushing off half-cocked to burn the guy's house down—that's a messy solution, not my style. No way to make it look like an accident."

"No, there's not." Mason pointed to the newspaper. "According to this, he was on vacation and just came home for a board meeting."

"He came back just to fuck with us?"

"Apparently."

"Why?"

"Why indeed. I guess he's a friend of the Bacchettis'."

"And this actress appealed to him for help?"

"Which she shouldn't have done, as I have told her in no uncertain terms."

Gerard frowned. "If he was just here for the meeting, why is he still in town?"

"Someone burned down his house."

"He didn't know that was going to happen. Why'd he stick around for it?"

"Are you saying he burned down his *own* house?"

"That's probably what the police are wondering, based on the fact that he survived. You did say he got out?"

"Yes."

"Was he injured?"

"Apparently not."

"Then someone didn't do a very good job. Assuming it was arson."

"The police aren't saying, but it sure sounds like it."

"What do you mean?"

"The police refused to comment. You can practically hear the reporter saying, 'The only reason I can't tell you it's arson is the cops are being hard-asses.'"

Gerard nodded. "So maybe he did burn it himself."

"Why?"

"To frame us."

"How? What connects us to the crime?"

"The fact that we'd profit from his death."

"You and I know that. No one else does. It makes no sense."

"Who else would want to burn down this guy's house?"

"Exactly."

S ammy Candelosi was pissed. "He got out?"

"Yes."

"You burned down his house. He was in it. And he escaped?"

"The guy is good."

"That's what everyone keeps telling me. That's not what I want to hear. I want to hear the guy is dead. Then he can be as good as he likes."

"I understand."

"This is not your first fire."

"No, it isn't."

Back in Jersey, Slythe had torched two houses belonging to a rival family. In neither instance had anyone escaped.

"So what happened?"

"It's not like I did anything wrong. I did everything right. I overprotected. I drenched that house with enough gasoline to burn down L.A."

"So where is he now?"

"I don't know."

"Find out."

Slythe called Centurion Pictures. "Billy Barnett, please."

"I'm sorry, Mr. Barnett's on vacation. Would you like to talk to his secretary?"

"Yes. Can you connect me?"

Moments later the secretary came on the line. "Billy Barnett's office."

"Could I speak to Mr. Barnett?"

"I'm sorry, he's on vacation. Could I take a message?"

"I need to speak to him directly. Could you ring him, please?"

"I'm sorry, that's not possible."

"Well, hang on, here. You say he's on vacation. According to the paper, his house burned down, and he was there at the time."

"That's right. Mr. Barnett has been on vacation all month. He returned temporarily for a board meeting, and while he was here his house burned down. He's put the matter in the hands of the police, and they are investigating. In the meantime, he's gone back on vacation. Which is actually convenient, since he has no place to live."

"How can he be reached?"

"He can't."

"And just where is he on vacation?"

Slythe could practically hear the smile in the secretary's voice. "If I told you that, he could be reached."

"I'm afraid my employers are not going to appreciate that answer. Can you help me?"

"If this is a matter relating to Centurion Pictures, I can put you in touch with someone else. If you have urgent personal business to discuss, I could refer you to his attorney."

"No, thank you."

"I'm sorry I can't be of more help. Would you like to leave a number?"

Slythe hung up the phone. "He's been on vacation all month, and no one's going to tell us where he is." He shook his head. "This is not good. Genaro hires an out-of-town hitter and the guy disappears."

"Hang on," Sammy said.

"What?"

"Something's not right."

"What do you mean?"

"They just told you Billy Barnett's been on vacation all month? That he came back for a board meeting, but aside from that he's been gone?"

"Yeah. So?"

"According to Jake, this cocktail waitress over at Pete Genaro's saw him on a movie set."

"Maybe it was a while ago."

"Didn't sound like it was a while ago. He was talking like it just happened."

"Maybe he got it wrong. The guy's not very bright."

Sammy nodded. "Let's ask him."

53

Jake felt like he was about to get whacked. He had no idea what he'd done to deserve it, but that only unsettled him further. He'd been summoned to Sammy's office, with no explanation, which couldn't be good. Even the curvy secretary looked foreboding. Now he was sitting in a chair in front of Sammy's desk, and no one was talking to him, and he was scared to ask why.

Then the door opened and Slythe came in, and he started saying his prayers.

Sammy picked up a newspaper from his desk and extended it to Slythe. "Show him."

Slythe took the newspaper and thrust it in front of Jake's face.

"What do you have to say about that?" Sammy demanded.

The newspaper was folded open to an article.

"'Producer escapes deadly blaze'?" Jake read.

"That's right."

"What about it?"

"You tell me."

Jake blinked uncomprehendingly. Getting no help from Sammy or Slythe, he looked back at the article. It read:

"Producer Billy Barnett, in town for a board meeting, nearly paid with his life. Mr. Barnett woke up in the middle of the night and smelled smoke. He was lucky he did. His house was gone minutes later."

Jake looked up to find Sammy glaring at him.

"This is the out-of-town hitter you warned me about?"

"That's his name."

"I know it's his name. Is it him?"

"Of course it's him. Who else would it be? Billy Barnett, movie producer."

"What studio was he with?"

"Oh, Christ, I don't remember."

"Centurion Pictures?"

"That's the one! Centurion Pictures!"

"Who told you that?"

"Bambi."

"Bambi?"

"One of Pete's bar girls. Said she saw him on the set of a movie. She was an extra, he was a stuntman."

"Stuntman? I thought he was a producer."

"She said he's working as a stuntman. She could have been wrong."

"About seeing him or about what he was doing?"

"I don't know. Could be either one. Could have been both."

"How could it be both?" Slythe said scathingly.

Sammy put up his hand. "This is kind of important information. When did she see him?"

"I don't know. It was before Pete hired him, because she gave him the idea."

"And when was that?"

"Just last week."

Sammy got up from his chair and came around the desk. Jake flinched, but Sammy got him to his feet and put his arm around him. "This is where you need to shine. You need to find out if Pete's still counting on this Billy Barnett to come help him. If an assassin is coming to kill me, this is information I need to know. You understand that. I need to know if the hit is still on, if this Billy Barnett is still a danger. According to the studio, he is on vacation. This is very bad news, particularly since they won't say where. So find out if the guy is here. Find out if Pete is expecting him."

"If I try to find out all that, Pete is going to know something's up."

"Pete thinks you're spying on me, right? So tell him I got a lot of firepower. Tell him you think he doesn't have enough. See if he reassures you he's taken steps to even the odds. You can do that, can't you?"

"Yeah, yeah. Sure, Sammy."

Sammy smiled, and stuck a finger in his face. "I've got big plans for you, Jake, you know that. As soon as Pete's out of the way, you will have a crucial role in running his casino. So you see how important this is."

"Yes, yes, of course."

"Good man." Sammy practically shoved him out the door.

"Well," Slythe said, "you think he can find anything out?"

Sammy grimaced. "Not a prayer."

54

Pete Genaro was at the end of his rope. A delivery truck servicing the casino restaurants had broken down, and six hundred pounds of prime meat, bought and paid for, had spoiled on the highway when the refrigeration unit also proved to have failed. Truly frustrating was that none of these "accidents" could be traced back to Sammy Candelosi, but everyone knew who was responsible. On top of everything else, Pete Genaro was becoming a laughingstock.

Pete called in Luke Fritz. He didn't want to do it. Luke was a scuzzy son of a bitch, the type of guy you didn't want to be seen with. Genaro didn't bring Luke into his office, lest he be spotted. He met him at an out-of-the-way diner where nobody he knew ever went.

Luke didn't want to be wined and dined at a fine restaurant, he just wanted the job. He ordered a grilled cheese sandwich. It was all he ever had.

"What you got?" Luke said.

"What do you charge these days?"

"Twenty-five grand, ten up front. No guarantees."

"Are you shitting me?"

Luke shrugged. "What can I tell you? Inflation."

"How soon can you do the job?"

"That depends what it is."

"Sammy Candelosi."

"No way."

"I figure it should be easy. It's not like it's out of town."

"Easy to say no," Luke said. "You know who Sammy Candelosi is?"

"If I didn't, I wouldn't be talking to you."

"If you did, you wouldn't be talking to me. Sammy Candelosi's connected. And when I say *connected*, I mean horsehead-in-your-bed connected. No way I mess with those guys."

"He's just one man."

"Bullshit. He never goes anywhere without his bodyguard, and he is one sick motherfucker. The type of guy whose pulse never rises while he cuts your throat."

"Are you trying to drive the price up?"

"Hell, no. All this meeting's costin' you is one sandwich. If Sammy Candelosi's buggin' you, just ignore him and hope he goes away. Because I won't mess with him, and I can't think of anyone who will."

Luke stood up. "Thanks for the sandwich."

P ete got back to his office in a foul mood. His curvy secretary tried to soothe him, but he was having none of it. She gave up and went back to manning the desk.

When Jake came in, she headed him off. "I don't think he wants to see you."

It was the type of response Jake had been getting lately, which was making it easier for him to shift his loyalties to Sammy Candelosi. Sammy had promised him big things, a role in running the casino—the kind of gig Jake had long since earned from Pete Genaro, as far as he was concerned. Unfortunately Sammy wanted information, and Pete didn't want to give him any. At least that was the way it seemed. Pete never came out and said he didn't want to bring Jake into the loop. Jake was just nervous about asking, and his broad hints were often so oblique as to go unnoticed.

Jake bit the bullet. "He sent for me," he said, and pushed his way in.

Pete Genaro clearly didn't want to see him. "What do you want?" he snarled.

"I thought you wanted to see me."

"Who told you that?"

Jake shrugged. "Got a message."

"Aw, fuck."

"What's the matter?" Jake said.

Pete leaned back in his chair and shook his head. "I've been running this place for fifteen years. I do a good job, everything's going great. And then some asshole moves in and blows it all to hell."

"What are you gonna do?" Jake said.

"I'm working on it. There will be a brief delay." That was the euphemism Pete had come up with to explain the fact that he was in over his head and didn't know what to do. "What's Sammy up to?" Pete asked.

Jake realized he was supposed to be spying on Sammy for Pete. He often lost sight of that in the shuffle. "Oh," Jake said, "he sabotaged your meat truck." Sammy had told Jake to reveal that to Pete.

"No shit," Pete said. "I could have told you that myself."

"Now you know for sure." Jake fidgeted. He had to push for information. "I thought you were bringing in outside help."

Pete glared up at him. "I told you there will be a delay."

"Yeah, sorry," Jake muttered.

Pete's blood pressure was boiling over. "Get out of here, willya?" It occurred to him he was particularly stressed. He called after Jake, "Send in Sherry."

55

Billy Barnett was not in Las Vegas plotting to kill Sammy Candelosi, nor did he have any intention of going. Billy Barnett, aka Mark Weldon, aka Teddy Fay, had enough on his plate. He was, temporarily, a man with three identities and no house.

While he could stay on at Stone Barrington's, at least until Stone returned for the next stockholders' meeting, the logistics of living so close to the studio and to the Arrington Hotel raised problems when it came to juggling identities. Just who was living at Stone Barrington's house? Billy Barnett, who was supposedly away on vacation? Mark Weldon, who had no connection to Stone Barrington whatsoever? Or Teddy Fay, who didn't exist?

The fact that people were trying to kill him merely complicated the problem.

Teddy didn't have time to shop around. He bought a house on Mulholland Drive, sight unseen—a modern three-story split-level built into the hillside, with a terrace and swimming pool. It was a little conspicuous for someone on the run, but for a producer as successful as Billy Barnett had recently become, a modest address would also stand out, so there was no reason for Teddy not to make himself comfortable.

Teddy had more than enough money in his offshore accounts to cover the purchase, though he had to be judicious about flaunting it. Teddy updated Billy Barnett's credit rating to arrange for the purchase.

Through Peter Barrington, Teddy hired renowned set dresser Marvin Kurtz to furnish it. Kurtz was given carte blanche, since Billy Barnett was on vacation at an undisclosed location and could not be reached.

Teddy also rented a one-bedroom apartment for stuntman Mark Weldon. From habit, he didn't rent it under Mark's name. No one knew where Mark Weldon lived, and Teddy saw no reason to change the situation. He didn't need to get mail there, and it never hurt to have another safe house. And that didn't stop him from being Mark Weldon as far as the tenants in the building were concerned.

Teddy ordered furniture and furnishings, and paid extra for rush delivery. He introduced himself to the super, Paco Alvarez, who lived in the basement apartment, explained that he was a stuntman on a movie and would be gone all day, and gave him a generous tip to accept delivery. He also ordered a computer delivered, and Internet service installed.

All this would take time, and Teddy needed a private place to lie low now.

Teddy drove back to Stone Barrington's house and changed his look from Mark Weldon to Billy Barnett. Then he drove out to the Santa Monica airport. Peter Barrington's hangar came with a small one-bedroom apartment. Teddy and his wife had lived there before moving into their house.

The pilot in charge of the hangar was working on the engine of Peter's plane when Teddy arrived.

"You don't have to look like you're busy every time someone walks in," Teddy said.

The pilot's eyes widened. "Mr. Barnett!"

"Billy."

"How are you?"

"Fine. How are you?"

"Your house burned down."

"That's why I'm here. I'd like to stay in the apartment a few days, if it's all right."

"It's your apartment."

"I assume it's undisturbed?"

"It's been cleaned once a week. Aside from that, no one's been in."

Teddy went upstairs and checked out the apartment. It felt like he'd been gone for ages, though actually it had been just a couple of years. The apartment was virtually bare. There were some shirts and pants, a sports jacket, and a pair of sneakers with no laces.

There were a few basic toiletries in the bathroom, like a toothbrush and toothpaste. There was of course no food. The computer was gone, and the Internet connection was disconnected.

Teddy made sure the water was running and the electricity was on.

Then he checked out the safe.

The safe in the airport apartment was neither as secure nor as large as the one in his house; still, it was a good quality product and virtually tamperproof. For most safecrackers nothing short of dynamite would have moved it.

Teddy spun the combination and swung open the door. The selection of handguns was meager but adequate. The lone sniper rifle was not handcrafted, merely a CIA-issued weapon in a case. And the collection of IDs and credentials was skimpy. It would do in a pinch, but not if a specific ID was needed. In this case, that was Billy Barnett. That ID was not there, because it was the one he always carried.

His duplicates had been in his house.

Well, that was something he would have to deal with. For now he was just happy to have a credit card. He chose James Haskell's American Express because his driver's license photo looked enough like either Billy Barnett or Mark Weldon that he wouldn't need to change his appearance to use it.

Teddy took out a shoulder holster and slipped it on.

He smiled.

It was nice to have a gun he didn't have to carry in a paper bag.

56

Peter was filming on location at the Merryweather Hotel in downtown L.A. when the cell phone was delivered. They were shooting stuntman Mark Weldon's perilous climb up the side of the building to the ledge outside the fourteenth-floor hotel room window, the companion piece to the scene they had already filmed on the soundstage at Centurion where Teddy could occasionally be seen in the background as he eavesdrops on Tessa and Brad. In this instance they were in the background, seen only briefly through the window as Teddy climbs up onto the ledge.

Unlike most sequences of this nature, where the shot of Teddy climbing up the building would later be intercut with a shot from the soundstage mock-up of him arriving on the ledge, Peter was shooting it for real. He had rigged a camera on a mechanical arm in an adjacent window that would catch the last flight of Teddy's climb, with the side of the building and the street below in the shot, and then extended out as the camera panned down and around to catch Teddy's arrival on the ledge from behind with the hotel room in the background.

It was a million-dollar shot for a big studio production, and Peter was bringing it in for next to nothing. The only downside was it required several takes to make sure the camera was aimed correctly.

Tessa was relaxing in her trailer while they filmed Teddy's climb when a production assistant knocked on the door to deliver a package that had just arrived by messenger.

Tessa knew it would be a cell phone, and managed to get rid of the production assistant before it rang.

"Yes?"

"Hello, Tessa. Have you been a good girl?"

"What do you want now?"

"Temper, temper." The voice was mocking. "You wouldn't want to make me mad."

"Why did you call?"

"Where's Billy Barnett?"

"You ought to know. You burned down his house."

"I didn't burn down his house."

"Then you had it done."

"I didn't do that either. I don't know why you have such a bad opinion of me."

"As if you care."

"Oh, I do care. If we're going to deal with each other, it's important that we're honest with each other. I'm honest with you. I said I have the video, and I have it. And I proved it. You say you don't know where Billy Barnett is. Can you prove it?"

"Obviously not. Start making sense or I'm hanging up."

"Oh, no, no, no, no. You don't tell me what to do. I tell you what to do. Now, here's the deal. I need to know where Billy Barnett is so I can tell what he plans to do. If he's away on vacation, that's fine, as long as he stays there. But if he heads for L.A., I will hold you personally responsible. If he shows up at the meeting, it will mean you're not cooperating and the game is over. We *will* post the video."

"I can't control what he does."

"Why not? I never knew a woman who couldn't get a man to do something if she wanted to. Offer whatever inducements you need, but make it happen."

The line clicked dead.

57

essa waited impatiently down below while Teddy scrambled up the side of the building. He was quick about it; still, it seemed to take forever. Finally he reached the window ledge and Peter yelled, "Cut." Peter was down in the street, talking over a bullhorn.

"Come on down, we're going again," Peter called. He lowered the bullhorn. "Tessa, after the next take we'll probably need you and Brad up there. It's a new setup, we'll tell you when."

Tessa nodded and moved off toward the catering cart to avoid getting into a conversation with Peter. She was too keyed up to talk about the scene.

When Teddy came out she waved him over.

"He called me again."

"What did he say?"

"Wanted to know where you are."

"What did you tell him?"

"I told him I didn't know."

"How'd that go over?"

"He didn't believe me."

"I don't blame him. What else did he want?"

"He said he didn't burn down your house."

"How did that come up? Did he just volunteer it?"

"No, I accused him of doing it. He said he didn't."

"Interesting."

"You think he didn't do it?"

"I think he's very good at playing the game. If I wanted to claim I didn't do it, that's what I'd say."

"Who else could it be?"

"Who burned down my house?"

"Yes."

"Any number of people might want to, but it had to be someone who knew I was there."

"And no one did?"

"I wouldn't say no one. I cover my tracks as best I can. There's always something you don't plan for."

"I'm worried about you."

"I can take care of myself."

"I know you can. But you lost everything in the fire. I'd feel better if you were armed."

Teddy pulled his jacket back and showed his shoulder holster.

"Ta-da!"

Tessa's eyes widened. "Where did you get that?"

"I'm a bad guy. Guns seem to find me."

"Is that a prop?"

"Of course it's a prop. Lighten up, will you, we gotta make a movie. This gun's a prop, but I actually have a gun. Believe it or not, it's the only thing I saved from the fire."

"I believe it. Good. I was worried. I drove by Stone's house last night and your car wasn't there."

"I moved out."

"To where?"

"An undisclosed location."

Tessa paused. "Well, I suppose it's better if I don't know."

58

Teddy pulled up in front of his house, or what was left of it. He parked on the street and walked up the drive, just an unfortunate owner inspecting the damage.

A crime-scene ribbon was strung in front of the rubble, due to the fact that the police were considering it arson. Teddy stepped over it and went up to the stoop. The front door was gone, indeed, as was most of the front wall. The remnants were no longer smoldering. There was no smoke. Except for the danger of falling debris or a floor cave-in, it was relatively safe.

Teddy walked through what had been the living room. Nothing remained. He checked where his office had been. His computer had melted from the heat. There was no hard drive for him to destroy.

Teddy was in luck. The firemen had managed to save part of an interior wall. It was worthless in itself, but it blocked the view from the street. Behind it was the real reason Teddy had come. The wall would protect him while he inspected it.

Teddy stepped around the corner to see if his incredibly expensive, state-of-the-art safe was really fireproof.

It was. The massive floor safe was covered with ashes and debris, but the titanium underneath had not dented, blistered, or in any other way succumbed to the heat.

Teddy crouched down out of sight from the street and went to work on the combination. The dial stuck a little, but the tumblers clicked. Teddy took a breath, and swung the door open.

The safe had stood up well. The Ziploc bags containing his sets of credentials had not melted. The bills in his cash supply were still crisp. The wigs and disguises and makeup kit appeared to be fine, too.

But all of that was incidental. Teddy's eyes were immediately drawn to the gun that had killed Ace Vargas. It was separate from his other weapons in its own evidence bag. He snatched it up and examined it. He breathed a sigh of relief. It was fine.

Teddy loaded the gun into the backpack he'd worn for that purpose. He put the bills and credentials in, too. He packed the wigs and disguises into trash bags he'd brought along in the backpack, and grabbed the makeup kit. He locked the safe, just in case he was interrupted and not able to get back, and toted everything to the car.

No neighbor came out to commiserate with him on the loss of his house, which was damn lucky, as he was dressed as Mark Weldon and had no right to be there.

Teddy locked everything in the trunk. He grabbed an empty backpack and a suitcase and hurried back to the safe. It opened easily—no sure thing when it stuck slightly once.

He'd cleaned out everything but the weapons, of which there were many. There was the sniper rifle he'd designed himself, with the silencer and the scope. It had its own case, but other things didn't. They included a wide variety of handguns, some with silencers, and some designed to be as noisy as possible. Some were huge. Some held only two shots but could fit in the palm of your hand.

Teddy had brought towels to wrap the hardware in. He filled the suitcase and the backpack.

There were still a number of burglar tools remaining, such as crowbars and wire cutters, but nothing that related directly to crime. Teddy grabbed the case with the sniper rifle, locked the safe, and toted the weapons back to the car.

He locked his arsenal in the trunk and exhaled in relief.

And looked around.

Teddy had another bag in his trunk that would hold the burglar tools, but entering the house a third time would be pushing it. He had everything crucial. He should drive away, thanking his lucky stars. But in the back of his mind he had a vision of a fire inspector and the head of the arson squad forcing him to open the safe in their presence, and then demanding to know why he had such a massive security device just to protect a few simple tools. Far better they find nothing to discuss.

Teddy grabbed the bag and hotfooted it back to the house. The lock stuck this time, wouldn't you know it, but he got it open and stashed the tools in his bag.

Teddy locked the safe and made a last perilous journey from the house to the car.

As he drove away from the house, waves of relief flooded over him. He had retrieved everything that had been in the safe. And now he had no reason to go back.

59

Teddy finished unloading the car into his hangar apartment and called Mike Freeman.

Mike was pleased to hear from him. "I hear your house burned down."

"Your vast network of spies?"

"I saw it on TV."

"I'm surprised I rated the coverage."

"There was a hint of arson."

"It was a pretty broad hint. At least a dozen empty gas cans were found at the scene."

"It's a wonder the police don't have you in handcuffs."

"Maybe they were stumped by my lack of motive. Burning it down while I was in it also struck them as a dumb move."

"Do they have any other suspects?"

"I doubt it."

"What about this Nigel Hightower the Third?"

"What about him?"

"Could he have done it?"

"In a word, no."

"Are you sure? It would be a relief. To know he's still alive."

"He's still alive, Mike. But he couldn't burn a house down unless it was a fraternity prank and someone else brought the matches. Trust me, it wasn't him."

"You know who it was, don't you?"

"I've got a pretty good idea."

"Are you going to do something about it?"

"Would you want to know if I did?"

"I guess I'd better hang on to my ignorance and plausible deniability," Mike said dryly.

"Probably better," Teddy agreed. "Anyway, I bought a house on Mulholland Drive."

"I heard that, too. Rather posh, I understand."

"It's a Hollywood house. Modern three-story split-level, with a terrace and a pool. I have no idea what security system is in there now, but it can't possibly be adequate. I'd like Strategic Services to install your top-of-the-line equipment."

"You haven't seen the security system?"

"I haven't seen the house."

"You're kidding."

"Billy Barnett's on vacation, and there's no reason to come back. Someone just tried to kill him. I'm hoping they won't burn down his house if he isn't in it, but I'd still like it armed. Can you do that for me?"

"You know I can."

"Your men will have to apply to the real estate agent to get in. I'll let her know they're coming."

"Do you want cameras?"

"Exterior only. I'm counting on you to make sure no one gets in. Also, figure out where to put a floor safe and get me the best you can find, fireproof, virtually impregnable, that can't be picked. Something in the neighborhood of six feet high and four feet wide."

"You're letting me design your house for you?"

"Good point. Your men may run into Marvin Kurtz, who is designing the house, and may be a little territorial. Tell them to go easy on him, but get the job done."

"You got it."

"Good man. Talk to you later."

"You need anything in the way of personal armaments?"

Teddy glanced at the array of weapons he'd just lugged up from the car.

"I'll be fine."

60

Jake reported back to Sammy Candelosi. He'd been putting it off because he figured Sammy wouldn't be happy.

He wasn't. "That's all you've got?"

"That's a lot, Sammy. He's bringing in out-of-town talent. The guy's been delayed, but he'll be coming. What more do you want?"

"Who's the guy? When's he coming? Where is he? Why is he delayed?"

"I thought you knew who the guy was."

Sammy's eyes widened. "You gonna argue with me?"

"Oh, no, of course not. All that would be good to confirm. But he didn't want to tell me. What am I going to do, say you gotta tell me, Pete, Sammy wants to know? I'm doing everything I can without tipping him off."

"Or you *already* tipped him off so he's not giving you anything."

"He doesn't suspect a thing, I swear."

"Then get back there and get me some more information.

And speed it up, will you? You took so long getting this I thought you were dead."

Jake said nothing, just stood there and took the abuse. He figured it could have been worse.

"Go on, get out of here," Sammy said.

Jake grimaced as he headed for the door. It seemed everyone was telling him that lately.

When he was gone, Slythe said, "What do you make of that?"

Sammy shrugged. "He's probably right. The guy's house burned down, and he's hung up dealing with it. When he gets his affairs in order, he'll be headed here."

"How long will that take?"

"Damned if I know. No one ever burned down my house."

"So he's still in L.A."

"It would appear so."

"You want me to go back and try to find him?"

"That might take a little time. I need you here."

"So what do you want to do about him?"

"There's guys who handle that sort of thing."

61

S kip tracer Tony Zito was a beefy ex-cop known for his uncanny ability to find people. Less well known was what he was willing to do to them once he found them.

Sammy Candelosi sized him up. The man didn't look like a private investigator. Square-jawed and paunchy, he looked like your run-of-the-mill goon.

"I understand you can find people."

"That's my job."

"Even people who don't want to be found."

"It's not hard finding people who *want* to be found."

Sammy chose not to regard the remark as insolent, though it certainly was. "You also deal with them."

"If they need to be dealt with."

"This man needs to be dealt with."

"I'll find him for ten thousand. I'll deal with him for twenty more."

"That's a lot of money."

Tony shrugged. "I can just find him and you can kill him yourself."

"I'm not a killer, Mr. Zito."

"No, you just hire them," Tony sneered. He was an obnoxious man, too dumb to know how unpleasant people found him. "I don't think the cops would like that either."

"Were you planning on turning me in?"

"Not if you pay me. Who's the guy?"

"A Hollywood producer named Billy Barnett."

"That the guy whose house burned down?"

"That's right."

"So, your man botched the job, and now you require the services of a freelancer."

Slythe's eyes burned fiercely. It was his only reaction.

"Will you do it?" Sammy said.

"This guy's in L.A.?"

"Last I heard."

"If I gotta fly around the country, it will cost you expenses."

"On top of thirty grand?"

"That's my price. We're talking expenses. You pay 'em."

"Fine. Barnett's been in L.A. a couple of years. He may have some hidey-holes around town you can check."

Tony Zito's look was withering. "You trying to tell me my job?"

Sammy's expression never changed, but he nodded to Slythe.

It happened fast. One moment Tony Zito was sitting there, and the next he was flat on his back. He came up sputtering with a gun in his hand.

Both men ignored the gun. Slythe said, "You obviously don't

know who Sammy Candelosi is. He's new in town, it's under-standable. You're allowed one mistake."

"I'm sure the man meant no offense," Sammy said. He put his arm around the skip tracer's shoulders and walked him toward the door. "I'm not trying to tell you your job, Mr. Zito. Show me that you know how to do it."

62

Teddy woke to the sound of breaking glass. He slipped out of bed with his gun in his hand and stepped into a pair of sneakers. He crept to the door. There was no sound behind it. He eased it open. There was no one on the stairs, but he could hear someone walking down below. The guy was clearly an amateur—he was making more noise than progress. Evidently he hadn't brought a light.

Whoever he was, he had no right to be there. Peter or the pilot wouldn't show up at two in the morning. If they did, they'd turn on a light. And they wouldn't break a window to get in.

The intruder was thrashing around. Teddy half expected to hear him knock over a carton of Coke bottles from the soda machine, a relic of past years. Cokes were still ten cents in the machine, a losing venture but well worth it just for the nostalgia.

The crash did not come, but a crackle of paper indicated he was making his way toward the stairs. Teddy didn't want him to get there. He grabbed a flashlight he always kept on the table by the door, slipped out, and crept down the stairs.

The intruder was almost there. Hoping the battery worked, Teddy clicked the flashlight on.

A beefy man with a gun in his hand blinked in the sudden light. His face was a picture of consternation. He tried to aim the gun.

Teddy shot him in the head.

The body fell on the gun with a heavy thud, but it didn't go off. That was the only thing Teddy had been afraid of, an unsilenced shot that would draw attention.

Teddy rolled him over and pried the gun out of his hand. He was a goon, your standard, card-carrying enforcer. Teddy had known enough of them in his day. This one was out of his league.

Teddy pulled out the goon's wallet and checked his ID. The man who'd tried to kill him was Tony Zito. He had a Las Vegas driver's license.

So, it looked like Mason Kimble and Gerard Cardigan had brought in out-of-town talent. That figured. Not knowing where he was, they'd hired a skip tracer. The fire starter had probably also been an import, though it probably hadn't been this guy. The guy who built the fire and failed to kill Teddy would hardly get a second chance.

Neither would Tony Zito.

Teddy went out to the parking lot and found the goon's car. It wasn't hard. It had a Nevada plate, and Teddy had the keys. He clicked the button and the lights flashed.

Teddy drove it around to the hangar, opened the bay door,

and pulled in. He popped the trunk and stuffed the dead man inside. He backed out of the hangar and closed the bay doors.

He had to ditch the car. He didn't want it found close to the airport, but he didn't feel like walking back either.

There were usually bicycles parked in front of one of the larger hangars across the way. Teddy checked to see if any were unlocked. None were, but he chose one with a flimsy lock he could pick in thirty seconds and threw it in the backseat of the car. He set off along the coast.

About five miles away he found what he wanted, a cliff overlooking the sea. He stopped the car and took out the bicycle. He hopped back in, put the car in gear, and headed it for the edge of the cliff. He gunned the motor and jumped out at the last moment.

It wasn't pretty. The car didn't have enough momentum to sail off the cliff. It just barely made it over, dropping straight down, striking the side of the cliff as it fell, landing upside down in the shallow water.

Teddy didn't wait to see if the tide would sweep it away. He just hopped on his bike and started back for the hangar.

As he rode he heaved a sigh. The dead hit man, easy as he'd been to take care of, posed a real problem.

Someone knew about Billy Barnett's airport apartment.

He'd have to move again.

63

Teddy checked with Paco Alvarez, the super at his apartment. Mark Weldon's bed and computer had been delivered, and his Internet service had been installed. His furniture hadn't all arrived, but that was enough. There was no reason not to move in.

Teddy loaded everything he had into the car. It wasn't much. His collection of guns and disguises from the safe made up the bulk of it.

The pilot arrived at the hangar while he was finishing up. "You moving out?"

"Yes, I am."

"I'll be sorry to see you go."

"This was only temporary, while I got back on my feet."

"Is your new house ready?"

"No, but I'm on vacation. I only stuck around to deal with the fire damage. My house will be ready by the time I get back."

"So you won't be using the apartment?"

"Only in emergencies. I hope we don't have any. I'll be around to fly."

"Are you getting a new plane to go with your new house?"

Teddy's turboprop was fine for short flights but wouldn't do for a cross-country trip. He borrowed Peter's jet on those occasions.

"I hadn't thought of it," Teddy said, "but that's an interesting idea."

Teddy hopped in the car and took off for his new apartment. He stopped off at Stone Barrington's house on the way. He didn't bother getting the key from the front desk at the Arrington Hotel, he just picked the lock. He went in, grabbed his makeup kit, and changed from Billy Barnett into Mark Weldon in case he encountered the super on his way into the apartment. The odds of that happening were good. Paco didn't stay in his apartment much, and could often be found hanging out on the stoop.

He was out there when Teddy pulled up.

Paco was trying to beat the heat by wearing a sleeveless undershirt, and sipping something cold from a paper bag in his lap.

"Hi, Paco."

"Hey, Mr. Weldon."

"Mark."

"You moving in?"

"If you could call it that. I haven't got much stuff."

"Well, you can't park here. But leave the keys with me while you unload. You won't get a ticket."

Teddy left his car with the super and lugged his bags up to his new apartment. Luckily in this town a guy moving into a cheap apartment with few belongings and no furniture wasn't conspicuous. Paco had clearly seen enough starving-artist types not to blink an eye.

When he came back downstairs to get his keys from the super, he said, "Listen, there's no lock on the hall closet. Any problem if I put a simple hasp and padlock on the door? I'll take it off when I move out."

"You can if you want to. We've never had a break-in, though. Someone stole a bicycle off the front porch once, but it shouldn't have been left there."

"Thanks."

Teddy drove around to a hardware store and bought the best hasp and padlock they had. He also bought a screwdriver and a small electric drill set.

He passed a supermarket on his way home, but he could shop for food later. Right now he wanted to get back.

He parked around the corner where Paco had told him, and took the hardware back to his new apartment. He was relieved to find his bags undisturbed underneath the bed where he'd hidden them.

Teddy took out the hasp and lined it up against the closet door. He plugged in the drill and drilled starter holes for the screws. He didn't need the screwdriver he bought. The drill had a screwdriver bit, so he was finished in no time.

Teddy lugged the bags with guns and disguises and money and IDs and tools and locked them up in the closet. It wasn't ideal, but it would have to do until his new house was finished and he could put them in the safe. Luckily, nobody would be looking for Mark Weldon.

He just prayed no one knew Mark Weldon was actually Billy Barnett.

64

Slythe came in with the newspaper. "Well, so much for your skip tracer."

"Oh?" Sammy said.

"He was found in the trunk of his car at the bottom of a ravine in Santa Monica."

"What?"

"Apparently the guy wasn't quite as good at his job as he thought he was."

"Dammit."

"This proves one thing, though."

"What's that?"

"Billy Barnett's still in L.A."

"Tidying up his affairs?"

"Not according to his secretary."

"So maybe he *is* a stuntman on a movie, like Genaro's bar girl said, and he can't leave until the shooting is over."

"When is that?"

"I don't know, but we can find out."

"How are we going to verify whether he's actually Billy Barnett?"

"All we have is Jake's version of the story. We should get it firsthand. Let me find out who this bar girl is."

S lythe put on a dress shirt and a suit and tie. He combed his long hair back and tucked it into the neck of his shirt. He took twenty thousand dollars' petty cash out of Sammy Candelosi's safe, hired a limousine, and had it drop him at the front door of Pete Genaro's New Desert Inn and Casino. He stepped out of the limo, slipped two hundred dollars into the hand of the concierge, and said, "I want a seat at the no-limit hold 'em table, and I don't like to wait. Can you make that happen?"

The concierge beamed. "You know I can."

Five minutes later Slythe was seated at the table with five thousand dollars' worth of chips in front of him, which he bet carelessly and often. After a half hour, during which he'd lost all his chips and bought in again twice, he called the pit boss over and palmed him a hundred-dollar bill.

"Could you see if Bambi's working?"

M arsha Quickly was doing well. With more and more bar girls defecting, there were fewer per shift, which meant more customers and more cash for her. Bambi was earning tips like she never had before, and even counting for inflation it was remarkably good. She rented a nice apartment outside of town and leased a modest American car.

The only thing she didn't have was a man. Oh, the customers hit on her, but the customers were suckers. She wouldn't date one of them in a million years. A high roller, maybe, but high rollers weren't waited on by bar girls, they were served by high-class girls in stylish gowns who catered to their every whim, which sometimes included getting a five-thousand-dollar Vera Wang ripped down the front.

Marsha was just filling a tray with drinks when the pit boss tapped her on the shoulder.

"There's a high roller looking for you."

M arsha flashed her hundred-watt smile across the dinner table. It wasn't often a high roller asked for her, and when one did he usually turned out to be a pig. This man was nicely dressed, and though there was something about him that gave the impression of a coiled snake, he was polite and their meal was pleasant. Of course, two cocktails and a bottle of champagne might have something to do with her opinion. Or perhaps it was the rack of lamb she was contemplating.

Just the idea of being served instead of serving had a great deal to do with her mood. She allowed her high roller to fill her glass and took a healthy sip.

"So," he said, "you're an actress?"

Something dinged in the back of Marsha's alcohol-addled brain. *Actress* was a red flag. Next he'd claim to be a producer, and hint at what he could do for her in the industry, in return for certain favors, of course. He seemed to be leading into it.

"Yes, I am."

"You work in pictures?"

"I have."

He smiled. "That's wonderful. I don't know a thing about making movies, but I've always found them fascinating. You must tell me all about it."

S lythe was smug. "Jake missed one small detail."

"Why am I not surprised?" Sammy said. "What is it?"

"Billy Barnett *is* working as a stuntman, but under the name Mark Weldon."

Sammy rolled his eyes. "Oh, for Christ's sake."

"That's why no one can find him. Billy Barnett isn't around, but Mark Weldon is. He's working on the picture, and he can't kill you until the movie's done shooting."

"When is that?"

"This is the last week. They're supposed to finish Friday. I can't find out if Mark Weldon's working that day, because I can't get ahold of a shooting schedule, but I will. If he's working on Friday, we've got until then. Not that I plan to wait. I don't know where he lives, but I know where he works. I'll find him on the set."

"You'll have a hundred witnesses."

"I'm not going to walk up and shoot him."

"What are you going to do?"

"I won't know until I know the terrain."

"You're going to L.A.?"

"I already booked the flight."

65

Gerard Cardigan closed the door with more than his usual force.

Mason Kimble looked up from his desk. "What's the matter with you?"

"I can't find Billy Barnett."

"That's not surprising. Someone burned down his house."

"And he bought another house, but he isn't in it. He isn't anywhere. All anyone will say is he's on vacation."

"Maybe he's on vacation."

"Someone burned down his house. You don't go on vacation when your house burns down."

"Why are you so concerned with finding Billy Barnett?"

"We don't want him at the stockholders' meeting."

"He's not going to be there."

"What makes you so sure?"

"I read Tessa Bacchetti the riot act. She knows what will happen if he shows up."

"And what is that? What are you going to do if he shows up? Post the video online? If you do that, you lose your leverage and you'll never get the studio. Is smearing the girl enough?"

"It's something. Revenge on Ben Bacchetti at the very least."

"Yes, and if that was all you wanted to do, you could have done it a long time ago. You've got a lot invested in this."

"You're looking for Billy Barnett so you can kill him?"

"It would certainly make life easier."

"It would if we had nothing to do with it."

"You have absolutely nothing to do with it, and neither do I. No one's going to ask us any questions. No one's going to know we were involved."

"Yes, if we're not involved."

"Well, that's what *I've* been doing. What have *you* been doing?"

"Lining up investors. With all our stock purchases, our capital is spread pretty thin. I've been lining up people willing to invest in a PG-13 picture. There's more of them than you'd think. I've secured commitments for more than two hundred thousand dollars in less than a week."

"Oh, you smooth-talking man. Are you going to make a PG-13 picture?"

"I certainly plan to. I couldn't tell you exactly when. If you want to continue your witch hunt, feel free. Meanwhile I'm making money, so don't act like I'm doing nothing."

"What about Little Miss Porn Star? You want to give her another scare?"

Mason nodded approvingly. "Just what I was thinking.

That's the problem with this two-week delay. It's like a reprieve. She feels like she's off the hook, that nothing's going to happen until the meeting."

"Exactly. So what do you want to do?"

"I was thinking we could leak a rumor to the tabloids. Nothing specific, just a hint that there might be dirty pictures in her past."

Gerard made a face. "You might as well put her video on the Internet. If the gossip columns hint of dirty pictures, the game's over and she wins. Her publicist can issue a statement that Tessa Tweed has never posed for a nude photo in her life, and if any exist they are the work of unscrupulous people who filmed her without her knowledge by the use of spycams. After that, you've completely lost your leverage."

"Do you have a better idea?"

Gerard smiled. "I might. You want to do me a favor?"

"What's that?"

"Set the machine up, would you? I want to copy a DVD."

66

Tessa Bacchetti turned down the covers and climbed into bed. It was only ten-thirty, but she had an early call.

Ben climbed into bed next to her. "Are we getting old, or are we just in the movie business?"

Tessa grinned at him. "I'm in the movie business. You're getting old."

"Ah, you saucy wench," Ben said, kissing her.

"Don't get excited. I really do have to get to sleep."

"Serves me right for becoming a producer. I could have been a used-car salesman."

"Be still, my beating heart," Tessa said. "What woman could possibly resist?"

Ben fluffed up his pillow. He frowned. "What's this?"

"What's what?"

Ben held up a clear plastic jewel case. "It's a CD-ROM or DVD or something. It's not labeled. It doesn't say what it is."

Tessa felt a cold chill. She didn't trust herself to speak.

"So how did it get under my pillow?" Ben said.

"I have no idea."

"Well, that's mighty odd. What could it possibly be?"

"Maybe it's some producer trying to attract your attention with a stunt, just someone pitching a project. They probably paid the gardener or someone to sneak it inside and make sure you'd find it. Throw it away."

"Don't be silly. If someone was ingenious enough to get past our security system and get in here, I want to know who it is."

Ben got up and walked toward the TV.

"Are you going to play it now?" Tessa tried to sound tired and put-upon, and to conceal her rising panic. It took every ounce of skill she possessed.

"Damn right I am."

"Honey, please. I've got to get up."

"Don't worry. It won't take more than a minute."

Ben clicked on the TV. He shoved the disc in the DVD slot and hit Play.

A color picture filled the screen.

Tessa tensed, but it was just a commercial. Ben hadn't switched the feed over from cable TV to Auxiliary. He did so now.

The color picture was replaced by crackling black and white, the type of blank screen before a dubbed recording came on.

Tessa clenched her fists. She *knew* she should have told Ben the truth, that secrecy was futile and somehow the situation would come back to haunt her. Now she would have no choice.

The video came on.

The picture was still black and white, but a map of Africa filled the screen. The names Humphrey Bogart, Ingrid Bergman, and Paul Henreid were imposed over it. They dissolved into the title CASABLANCA.

"Look," Ben said. "*Casablanca*. Why would anyone send me this?"

"I have no idea," Tessa said.

"Maybe the housekeeper? She may have heard me mention it. Well, whoever it is, they have excellent taste. It's one of my favorite films."

Ben settled up against the pillows.

"You're going to watch it?" Tessa said.

"I'll keep it low."

"Oh, honey."

"Turn over. Go to sleep. I'll probably fall asleep in the first few minutes. I just want to watch."

Tessa pretended to sleep but couldn't. She knew in her heart the DVD hadn't been left by their kindly housekeeper, or even snuck in by an ambitious producer. She lay there on her side, her back toward Ben, watching the TV sideways, out of the corner of her eye. Occasionally she managed to turn in her feigned sleep enough to tell that Ben was still awake watching the movie.

It was excruciating. Tessa lay there, in the dark, bracing herself against the moment the TV screen would suddenly burst into living color, and there she would be, naked to the world.

It never happened.

But it didn't matter.

By the time Bogie finally said, "Louis, I think this is the beginning of a beautiful friendship," and walked off with Claude Rains, Tessa was a nervous wreck.

67

There was a cell phone in her trailer the next morning. Tessa had sensed there would be. It rang as she came in.

The voice, as usual, was mocking. "Did you enjoy the movie?"

"You son of a bitch!"

"Is that any way to talk? I give you a nice movie to watch, and this is the thanks I get?"

"What are you trying to do?"

"I'm not trying to do anything. Are you trying to do something? You shouldn't be. I wouldn't like that very much."

Tessa said nothing.

"I hope you don't get the idea that you're off the hook. You've got a lot to worry about, like the next DVD, for instance. You got any requests? How about *The Lady Vanishes*? That's a good one. Pretty appropriate, don't you think, the way your career is going to vanish if you don't play ball. Wanna watch that one and see if it runs straight through without any 'commercial interruption'?"

"Stay out of my house!"

"That was just a stunt. Shall I send it to your husband by old-fashioned snail mail? I will if it comes to that. But I don't think it will. I trust we understand each other."

Tessa listened in helpless fury.

Her tormentor chuckled. "Here's looking at you, kid," he said, and hung up.

68

Teddy had lunch with Peter Barrington. They couldn't do it as often as when he was producer Billy Barnett, but Peter could eat with his stuntman occasionally. They chose an out-of-the-way café five minutes from the studio that featured good burgers and fast service.

There was a lot to catch up on. Peter thought he was still living at the airport. Teddy hadn't told anybody about the break-in at the hangar, because there was no way to conveniently explain how he'd dealt with it. He just told Peter his apartment was ready.

"When will your new *house* be ready?"

"Ask Marvin Kurtz. I have no idea."

"You can move in next week when we wrap the picture and Billy Barnett gets back from vacation." Peter took a bite of his burger. "Are you ready for the money shot?"

The climax of the movie was being shot on the top of a construction site with bare steel girders. What Peter was referring to as the money shot was a shoot-out on top of the girders and a five-story fall.

"Not to tell you your business," Teddy said, "but on most pictures they schedule the crucial exteriors *early* in the shoot, in case there's bad weather and they have to move to the cover set and reschedule."

"Yes, and that's how I had it originally scheduled," Peter said. "Until I found out my featured villain would be doing his own stunt. I scheduled it at the end so in case you kill yourself falling off the beam, I can still cut the picture."

"You're all heart."

"I wish you'd use a stuntman."

"I *am* a stuntman."

"After the life you've led, to kill yourself making a movie would be pretty ironic."

Teddy smiled. "Hey, getting shot in the chest on a twelve-inch-wide steel girder five stories up in the air. What could possibly go wrong?"

69

S lythe, wearing a Hawaiian shirt and a pair of sunglasses, a camera hanging around his neck, stood in line for the Centurion Studios back-lot tour. He didn't have a reservation, but he bought a place in line for a hundred dollars from a college kid who was happy to have the money, and joined the group of starstruck tourists being led through the Centurion gate onto the lot.

Their guide was a young production assistant with an insider's arrogance and enough knowledge to get by.

"Now then," he said, "we're going to be walking through the sets where we shoot our street scenes. You may recognize them from the movies and TV. The same streets have appeared in many movies, slightly redressed, with different street signs, different windows, a different saloon door."

"Saloon door?" a big man in a straw hat said. He had a booming voice, louder than that of the guide's. "We're in New York City."

They were indeed walking down a Manhattan street, easily recognizable by the police station with an NYPD police car parked out front.

"Yes, we are," the guide said, "but if we turn right at the corner, I think you'll get the idea."

They did, and found themselves in front of a charming French café with tables on the street. A scene from *An American in Paris* could have easily been filmed there.

"See? Another street, another country, another time period. Our saloon door should be up on the left."

The group turned another corner and found themselves on a dusty street with hitching posts and water troughs, a saloon, a hotel, and a sheriff's office.

"There you go," the guide said. "Throw in a few horses and extras, and you're set for your gunfight at high noon."

"Where are the actors?" a girl wanted to know. She was of high school age, and clutched an autograph book.

The guide smiled. "Of course, everyone wants to see the actors. I'm afraid they're filming inside today. We can't enter the studio, but you might see someone on the way to their trailer or going out to lunch."

As if on cue, a man rounded the corner and came walking down the street.

"And look who that is," the guide said.

People craned their necks eagerly, whispering guesses as to who it was.

"That's special-effects wizard Fred Russell," the guide announced, and the crowd deflated. A technical wizard was not who they wanted to see. "Hey, Russell, how's it going?"

"Busy, busy, busy," Russell said, strolling up. "This film has a lot of special effects."

"What are you working on now?"

Russell had clearly done this many times and had his own line of canned patter. "This film has a zillion gunshots. For a contemporary thriller that's not a cops-and-robbers, that's rare. You can't shoot live bullets at the actors, because they're expensive to replace. We do it with blanks and squibs. If someone gets shot, it looks like they've been shot, but they can get up and walk off the set. I'm responsible for every gunshot in the movie. If there's one live round, I lose my job. And it's not great for the actor either." He smiled and raised his eyebrows at the joke, which landed with a thud.

Russell was carrying a bag. He set it down on the empty water trough and took out a gun. "Here's your basic gun. A .38 Smith & Wesson revolver." He swung open the cylinder and took out the shells. "And here's your bullets. You can see they're all blanks. Just a shell and a charge." He reached in his bag again. "And here's a live round. You can easily tell the difference because you can see the top of the rounded bullet." Russell reloaded the barrel and snapped it closed. "And there you are. A perfectly safe, personally inspected movie prop."

The man in the straw hat wasn't buying it. "Can I see the other bullet?"

"Oh, I put it away," Russell said. "But, trust me, it's perfectly safe. I stand behind my work. Actually, I stand in front of it. I can't let any gun be aimed at an actor that I wouldn't have aimed at me." He looked over the crowd. "Who wants to shoot me?"

"I do," the man in the straw hat said.

The guide chuckled and returned to his tour script. "I'm sorry to be a party pooper, but for insurance purposes we can't let any guest fire a gun on the property. *I'll* shoot Russell."

The guide took the gun and stepped out in the street. Russell stepped out and faced him. "Think you can hit me from fifteen feet?"

"I'll give it my best shot."

The schoolgirl giggled nervously.

"And draw!"

Russell drew an imaginary gun and aimed his finger.

The guide fired.

Blood gushed from Russell's chest. He jerked backward and collapsed in a heap.

There were gasps of shock and awe.

"Oh, my God!" the guide said. He rushed to the fallen man.

Russell leaped to his feet with a ta-da! gesture. "And he's still alive!" he declared. "Movie magic. You knew it was coming and you still bought it. That's why I showed you the real bullet. So in your mind, for a split second, you'd think I mixed them up." He pointed to his bloody shirt. "It's a blood bag and a squib, of course. I set it off with a detonator in my pocket. Pretty neat, huh?"

The tour group applauded halfheartedly. It was good theater, but it wasn't making up for the fact that there were no actors.

"So when do we see the cast?" Slythe said.

"I told you," the guide said, "they're filming inside today." A chorus of disappointed murmurs coursed through the crowd.

The guide continued, "But if you're still in town tomorrow, they'll be shooting outside in the vicinity of Sunset and Main, on a construction site. Russell will be working, because they're actually filming a gunfight on a five-story-high steel girder. That's a shoot-out between Devon and Leonard Kirk."

The schoolgirl wasn't impressed. "Who?" she said.

"Those are the names of the characters in the movie. Leonard Kirk is an actor named Mark Weldon. And Devon"—the guide drew it out, teasing her—"is the star of the movie, Brad Hunter!"

There were oohs and aahs. The schoolgirl practically swooned.

"Hang on," Slythe said. "That won't be the actors. That will just be stuntmen."

The guide put up his hands. "Brad Hunter's scene on the high beam will be shot with a stuntman. Mark Weldon *is* a stuntman, so will perform himself. But Brad and Mark will both shoot the same scene on a low girder just a few feet off the ground. They'll actually shoot most of it there. The high beam is just for the stunt."

"And what's the stunt?" Slythe wanted to know.

"Oh. Brad shoots the bad guy, and he falls off the beam, down five stories to his death."

Slythe smiled. "No kidding."

70

Slythe was waiting in his rental car outside the Centurion gates when the shift ended. After a few minutes Russell came out talking and laughing with a couple of production-crew types. They hopped into their cars and took off.

Slythe followed them a few miles down the road to a workingman's bar, complete with shuffleboard and a pool table. All were greeted by the bartender and ordered draft beer.

Slythe bellied up to the bar and ordered one, too. He was in luck. Russell's buddies started shooting pool.

Slythe slapped a goofy grin on his face and pointed. "Hey, aren't you the guy?"

Russell grinned. Clearly this had happened to him before.

"The gun guy with the special effects. From the movies? That was you."

"You were on the tour."

"Damn right. Is that part of the job? You gotta do the tour when you're not on the set?"

Russell grinned. "You a cop? No, it's not part of the job. They slip me a little on the side to entertain the tourists. It's hokey, but they gotta give them something to make up for not seeing the actors."

"No offense, but it doesn't."

"No kidding. Well, tomorrow I don't have to do it."

"You're working the construction site?"

"That's right."

"Do you have to go up on the high beam?"

"I hope not. I'm hoping I can check their guns on the ground, before they go up and shoot the scene."

"What time do you think they'll shoot it?"

"It should be the first shot. If they can't get that, there's no point shooting the other stuff."

"What if it doesn't work?"

"The director will figure out something else that *does* work, and shoot that. And the stuff on the ground will be shot to match. If you shoot the stuff on the ground first and the stunt doesn't work, you're screwed. Nothing will match."

"What do you mean the stuff on the ground? I thought the scene was five stories up."

"They'll shoot some of the scene on a lower beam a couple of feet off the ground, so they can get some shots with the actors' faces. They won't put them at risk doing the actual stunts. The stuntmen practice on it, too, to get the footwork right. Running on a narrow beam isn't easy."

"Will they be using the same gun you were using today?"

Russell snorted. "Hardly. The bad guy will be using a .38 snub-nosed revolver, but Brad will be using a Sig Sauer P320 nine millimeter. He thinks it looks stylish. Can you imagine that? Stylish. All that means is some other actor used it in some other movie and he wants to be like him."

"Are you saying the guy's an asshole?"

"Absolutely not, and you didn't hear it here." Russell set his empty glass on the bar. "Guess I better go. Six AM call with the prop man, and he'll bust my chops if I'm late."

"He a hard-ass?"

"Sometimes, when he's stressed. Tomorrow's a big job—we gotta load our supplies and get to location by seven AM to be ready for shooting."

"No sweat, then. Take it easy. Have one on me." Slythe tossed money on the bar, said, "Give this man another beer," and went out.

Slythe got in his car and checked his cell phone to see if Fred Russell's address was listed. It was. Good.

He wouldn't have to follow him home.

71

Winston Sporting Goods had very poor security for a place that sold guns. Slythe had no problem disconnecting the alarm system, smashing a bathroom window, and letting himself in.

With a pencil flashlight he made his way to the firearms section. He was pleased to see a Sig Sauer among the guns hanging on the wall. He didn't take it, but began pulling out drawers below the countertop. They held nothing but bullets, from BBs to buckshot to assault rifle magazines.

In the middle drawer he found what he wanted: a box of 9mm cartridges. He opened the box and dumped a pile of bullets out on the counter. He took the Sig Sauer off the wall and loaded it just to make sure they fit.

When he was done he popped the magazine, thumbed out the bullets, and ejected the one in the chamber. He slid the empty magazine into the gun and hung the Sig Sauer back on the wall.

He put a dozen bullets in his pocket and returned the rest to the box. He closed the box and put it back in the drawer, underneath another box of identical shells.

He swept up the glass, locked the bathroom window, and went out the back fire door, pulling it shut behind him. He reset the security alarm, hopped in his car, and drove off.

It couldn't have gone better. With luck, no one would notice there'd been a robbery. Certainly not before tomorrow.

After that it wouldn't matter.

Fred Russell was up at five o'clock. It was a huge tech day, and he had to be at the studio at six, and the set wasn't at the studio—it was at the top of a five-story-high construction site. A technician's nightmare to set up.

He pulled on a T-shirt, a pair of jeans, and running shoes, his standard attire. He didn't stop for breakfast, he'd get coffee and a Danish from the catering truck on the set. He checked that he had his money, his keys, and his wallet. He pulled on his cap and opened the front door.

A man stood in the doorway. He seemed vaguely familiar, but Russell couldn't place him. He was dressed in a T-shirt and jeans, with a baseball cap worn backward. Otherwise—

Russell's eyes widened.

The man from the bar.

The man Russell had just recognized stepped in with a straight razor and cut his throat.

72

Slythe drove down to Centurion and bluffed his way onto the back lot. It wasn't hard. The guard at the gate was half asleep and not expecting to do anything but check IDs.

"Who?" he said.

"Tim Dale. I'm supposed to check in with the prop department."

"No one said anything about it."

"I was just called in, someone phoned in sick. The union sent me instead."

"I don't know . . . "

"There's a big shoot today, and they told me to get my ass down here and report in. If they lose a day shooting they'll be blaming me. You know how it goes with these types," Slythe said, trying to appear like just another blue-collar guy who worked among a lot of people with more power and money than he'd ever have. "Who's the head of props?"

The guard picked up the phone. For a moment Slythe was

afraid he was calling the union to check up on him, but he was actually calling a production assistant to drive him to the set.

Slythe reported to the head of the prop department, who wasn't pleased to see him. Leon Gerber was a small, wiry man, always suspicious that someone was after his job. "What are you doing here?" he demanded.

"The union sent me to fill in for Fred Russell."

"No one told me."

"It just happened."

"Why'd they send you?"

"I answered the phone."

Leon snorted in disgust. "We have a tech-heavy shoot on location at a high-rise construction site. A shoot-out on a five-story-high girder, between a bad guy and the star. I can't tell you how important this is."

"Where's the equipment?"

Leon unlocked the prop room. As Slythe expected, the weapons to be used that day were laid out on the prop table. There were two guns, two boxes of blank cartridges, and two dozen squibs and blood bags.

"Don't tell me," Slythe said. "The star's using the Sig Sauer. The snub-nosed revolver is the evil bad guy's gun." He cocked his head at the prop man.

Leon smiled. "You'll do."

Slythe caught a ride to the location with some of the other prop men. No one cared about him much, and when he told them he hadn't done a feature in years, they left him alone.

That was good because one of them was one of the guys who'd been playing pool in the bar while he was talking to Russell. Luckily, the man clearly didn't recognize him.

They got to the set to find Leon already standing on the sidewalk. Slythe walked up to him and said, "Where are we setting up props?"

Leon said, "There's a table in the crew trailer where you can spread everything out, and someone will always be assigned to watch them."

"Who did Russell have doing squibs?"

"Jackson."

"He can do them today, then. I'll load the guns myself."

"We got a guy to load them for you."

"It's my first day. If something goes wrong, it's on me. I'll load them myself. Where's the trailer?"

"Show him, Jackson."

A teamster handed down a box of equipment from the truck. A prop man took it and said, "Come on."

Slythe followed him to the crew trailer, where the props department had been allotted the kitchen table to spread out the day's props.

The prop man unloaded the guns and cartridges and squibs onto the table.

"Where are the backup guns?" Slythe said.

"On the truck. We won't bring them out unless something's wrong with these."

"Are you the guy who does squibs?"

"Yeah, I'm Jackson."

"Good. You'll be doing them today. I'll check them, of course, but you rig them. Just let me know when you're done."

"There's only one squib."

"One?"

"Only one guy gets shot."

"Who's that?"

"The bad guy. The star shoots the bad guy. He doesn't get touched himself, so there's only one squib. You don't need any help with the guns?"

Slythe picked up the Sig Sauer, popped the magazine, checked that there was no round in the chamber. "Let's see. Sig Sauer, nine millimeter. Looks like a P320. And a snub-nosed revolver. Any other weapons?"

"Not today."

"Then I'm all set."

73

Teddy was on alert driving to the set. Mason Kimble and Gerard Cardigan weren't the type to give up. There was no indication that they'd pierced the Mark Weldon disguise, but he hadn't survived this long by assuming the best-case scenario.

Today was a day of maximum exposure. They weren't filming in the studio but were out on the street on location, and anyone could watch. The police would keep the crowds back, but anyone with a sniper rifle could take him out and he'd never see it coming.

Particularly when he was up on the beam, all alone, totally exposed. It was a city block with tall buildings on both sides of the street, a zillion places a gunman could be hiding.

Of course, he would have to know the shooting schedule, the location, the shot, and the script. They would have to know what actor was in which position at what time. True, Mason Kimble and Gerard Cardigan were movie people and would be familiar with location filming, but they would need to have someone on the inside feeding them the specifics.

Teddy realized he was being paranoid, but these guys had sent a hit man after him and burned down his house.

Teddy parked on the street, where production assistants were manning the four blocks with No PARKING signs that the police had posted in accordance with their permit. He got a coffee and a scone from the catering truck, and took them to the actors' trailer.

Tessa and Brad had their own trailers on location, but Teddy shared his with the other actors. Today that was only George, the stuntman who'd be playing Brad on the high beam. George was sitting at the makeup table with a paper cup of coffee.

Teddy slid in next to him. "Hey, George, how's it going?"

George grinned. "Ah, the man I get to shoot."

"Assuming your aim's good."

"It should be. We've rehearsed the scene enough."

The scene was simple. George, trapped on top of the construction site, runs out on a girder to escape. Teddy follows, stops, and shoots. The bullet whistles by George's head. George spins and shoots Teddy in the chest, knocking him off the girder.

Peter had built a mock-up of the girder in the studio to work out the moves for the gunfight. Teddy and George had run it enough times to be as confident on the twelve-inch-wide beam as any Olympic gymnast.

"We've rehearsed it three feet off the ground," Teddy said. "This is a little different."

"No kidding. Have you ever done stunt work on a high bar?"

"No, but a job's a job."

"I still don't get why you're doing your own stunts. You have a featured part, you don't have to do this shit."

"This shit is what I do. The acting's the stretch."

Peter stuck his head in the door. "Hey, guys. Ready to get your feet wet?"

Teddy grinned. "Ready when you are, C.B.," he said, paraphrasing the famous response of a cameraman to Cecil B. DeMille when asked if he had gotten the million-dollar action sequence that had just taken place on film.

"Okay," Peter said. "The landing balloon is all filled. Let's go jump."

"You realize I don't fall off the beam," George said.

"Not in the scene," Peter said. "But if you slip and fall, I'd rather you weren't killed."

"Thanks a lot."

"If you're thinking about the height, it will inhibit you. And then you could fall, because you're afraid you will. All we're doing is taking away the fear, showing you that if you *do* fall, it's all right."

"All right with *you*," George said.

Teddy and Peter laughed.

74

Kenny, the key grip, took them up in the elevator. The grips were responsible for any equipment on the set that had to be moved, and the construction elevator counted because it was in the shot.

Kenny ran them up to the top. "Fifth floor. Everybody out," he said, and opened the door.

Teddy, Peter, and George stepped onto the platform. The floor area around the elevator was not extensive. For the most part, it was just bare girders.

Peter nodded in satisfaction. "Perfect, just like we laid it out in rehearsal. Mark traps George up here, George goes out on the beam to escape. It's this one here to the right, with a clear shot down to the safety balloon. How does it look, Mark?"

"Fine."

"George, how does it look to you?"

"High. That balloon looks pretty small from up here," George said.

Peter smiled. "It's fifty feet wide. Mark, do you want to do the honors?"

"My pleasure," Teddy said.

He walked out on the girder, turned and waved, and hopped off.

The landing balloon was thick. Teddy never came close to touching the ground. He landed on his back, bounced, and settled. He crawled to the side, grabbed the thick rope around the perimeter of the balloon, and shimmied to the ground.

He stood up and waved. "Come on down!"

"Well, here goes nothing," George said.

He walked out on the beam and jumped. Seconds later he was scrambling to the side and lowering himself down next to Teddy.

"Well, how was that?" Teddy said.

George grinned. "Can we do it again?"

75

S lythe watched the practice jumps from his vantage point next to the catering cart. It was nice to see where the shot would be filmed, though he had no intention of going up there.

It was also nice to see where his quarry was going to fall.

Slythe didn't recognize either of the actors. He knew one was Billy Barnett, but he couldn't tell which.

Fortunately, it didn't matter.

One of the assistant directors, who had been waiting on the ground for the actors to make the jump, came walking up for a jelly doughnut.

"Will they be doing that again?" Slythe said, jerking his thumb in the direction of the jump.

"No, they're done," the AD said. "I took them to wardrobe and makeup."

"Anybody else going to jump?"

"Why, do you want to?"

"No way. But is anyone else?"

"Not likely. You know the type of insurance risk it would be for someone in the crew goofing around?"

"So that's it till the shot?"

"Should be."

Slythe finished his coffee. He crumpled his cardboard cup, tossed it in the garbage, and wandered off in the direction of the Porta-Potties. He detoured around them and strolled casually in the direction of the landing balloon.

Up close it was enormous. Slythe couldn't even see over the top.

Slythe glanced around. Back in the street, the crew was still unloading the trucks. Cameras, lights, and reflectors were being set up. Huge lights on tripods were being braced with sandbags.

No one was paying any attention to him. Still, he was within sight lines. He strolled around toward the far side of the landing balloon.

A policeman was standing there.

Slythe managed a smile. "Hey, how's it going?"

"Okay. You with the crew?"

"Props. You guarding the set?"

"I'm on traffic control, but there's nothing to stop until they begin filming. You know when they might start?"

"Not for a while. They're still setting up. You know, there's coffee over there—doughnuts, cheese Danish—if you wanna grab something."

"Not a bad idea," the cop said.

Slythe watched him go. He reached in his pocket, slid out his straight razor, and flipped it open.

He stepped up to the balloon.

"Tim!"

Slythe froze. His hand with the razor dropped to his side. He turned calmly, a seasoned pro, ready to size up the situation and react.

It was only Jackson. And he didn't look alarmed.

"What's up?" Slythe said.

"The director wants to see you."

76

eter Barrington sized Slythe up. "You're filling in for Russell?"

"That's right. I'm sorry if I'm not up to speed, but I just got the call. As I understand it, you're filming a gunfight on an I-beam."

"That's right. We're shooting the stunt up there, then close-ups later on a low beam. I'm particularly concerned with the shot up there. It's the first shot of the day. We'll have four cameras rolling. The villain shoots three times before the hero spins around and blasts him, and he falls. I'd like to get it in one take because it's a huge setup and I don't want the actor to have to do the fall twice. I need you to check the guns carefully just before the shot to make sure everything is in order."

Slythe pointed. "Up there?"

Peter frowned. "You have a fear of heights?"

"I don't like them. Do I have to be up there?"

Peter considered. "Well, Jackson has to be up there to set off the squib. But the guns . . ."

"Can't I just give them to the actors before they go up?"

"They have their guns in their shoulder holsters for the wardrobe check. Tell you what. How about you check them just before they get into the construction elevator?"

"Great. Thanks."

Slythe smiled.

Perfect.

77

Teddy nearly fell asleep in his makeup chair. He'd been on the go so much lately and the movie trailer was a safe space, a place where he could zone out and relax.

Teddy snapped awake when they came back to check his squib. Something was different, and he was attuned to notice anything out of the ordinary. He knew what it was immediately: the prop man. The guy checking his squib wasn't Russell.

"You're new," Teddy said.

The prop man nodded. "Tim Dale. Russell phoned in sick. Help me out here. If you're the guy with the squib, you must get this." He held out the snub-nosed revolver.

"Right you are," Teddy said. He took the gun, flipped it open, and spun the cylinder. He flipped it shut and stuck it in his shoulder holster. "I'm Mark. That's George. He gets the other one."

"Here you go."

George took the Sig Sauer and slipped it into his shoulder holster.

The prop man went out.

Teddy relaxed, relieved that the thing that had him on guard was something as simple as that.

Even so.

"Hey, George," Teddy said.

"Huh?"

"Let me see your gun."

"Why?"

"Just curious. After all, you're going to shoot me with it."

George handed over the gun.

Teddy popped the magazine and checked the blanks. He ejected the shell in the chamber. It was a blank, too.

Teddy stuck the magazine back in the gun, chambered the round, and handed the gun back to George.

Teddy felt foolish, but only a little. You didn't need doubts in your mind when you were five stories up on a twelve-inch-wide girder, about to fall off.

78

S lythe came out of the trailer feeling good. He'd carried off his masquerade as a prop man well enough to fool the director and both actors, including the one who was presumably Billy Barnett. Slythe wondered if he really was. He didn't look much like the man he'd seen emerge from the burning house, but that man had been a fright. This man was in costume and makeup.

But it had to be him. According to the bar girl, Mark Weldon was Billy Barnett, and she had been trying to impress him with her insider knowledge, and too drunk to lie.

Slythe glanced around. No one was paying any attention to him, nor was there any reason why they should. He'd done his job. No one would need him again until they were ready for the shot. He was on his own.

Slythe walked over to the landing balloon. The cop was back, but some of his buddies had arrived, and they were out in the street, probably planning traffic flow. No one seemed the least bit interested in a prop man hanging out between tasks.

Slythe slipped his razor out of his pocket and cut a twelve-inch horizontal slit in the side of the landing balloon. He stepped back to inspect the damage. Air was hissing out slowly. The balloon was deflating, not so fast that it would be noticeable too soon, but not so slowly that it wouldn't do its job.

Slythe walked all around the balloon, adding a cut here and there, before heading back to the catering cart for a coffee.

79

P laces, please!"

The assistant directors hurried around importantly, banging on doors and summoning everyone to the set. Or rather to the base of the construction site. The actual set was on the fifth floor, but no one was up there yet.

The people going up were gathered by the construction elevator. There weren't many—just the two stuntmen, the director, the cameraman, and Jackson on squibs.

Slythe was there, too, but he wasn't going up.

"Okay, guys, let's check those guns," Slythe said.

The stuntman who was presumably Billy Barnett handed over his snub-nosed revolver. Slythe popped the cylinder and checked the blanks, though he couldn't have cared less about them.

"Fine," he said. He snapped the gun closed and handed it back.

"And yours."

George handed over the gun. Slythe popped the magazine.

It was full, except for the shell in the chamber. He ejected the shell. It was the blank he'd loaded a half hour before. He palmed it and substituted one of the live rounds he'd stolen from the hardware store. He shoved it into the magazine. He popped the magazine into the gun and chambered the live round.

He smiled and handed the gun back to George.

"All set," he said.

80

Kenny took them up in the elevator. He'd taught George how to run the elevator for the shot, but union rules said the key grip had to bring up the crew. Otherwise there was no reason George couldn't have done it. The mechanism was simple: a handle stuck out the top of a semicircular casing and you pulled it to the right to go up; you pushed it to the left to go down.

This time everyone got off on the fourth floor. It was a little more finished than the fifth, but mostly just steel girders.

"Okay," Peter said. "This is where we all start. Dennis is on the camera. Jackson, you'll be right beside the camera with me. It's open air, no obstruction, you can set off the squib from there. Kenny, you're kind of trapped up here. Stay next to Jackson.

"Starting positions for the actors are George in the elevator, and Mark clinging to the side. But don't take them until we're set. George, do you want to take the elevator up and down a couple of times before we go?"

"I think I've got it."

"Do it anyway. I don't want to have four cameras rolling and have the elevator go down when it should go up."

"Okay."

George took the elevator up and down and announced that he was comfortable.

"Great," Peter said. "Let's try one."

Peter had a walkie-talkie. "Okay," he said to the first assistant director, who was on the ground. "Lock it up."

"Lock it up," the first AD yelled. "Lock it up!"

The sound mixer rang a bell as loud as a fire alarm. That was the signal for everyone to stop what they were doing and be quiet for the shot. It was also a signal for the policemen to stop traffic and keep the crowd back.

"Are we ready?" Peter said. "Okay, places, please. George into the elevator, Mark onto the side. All right, this is a take, we are going for picture. Roll it!" he said to his cameraman and into the walkie-talkie.

On the ground the first AD said, "Roll it!" to the other cameramen.

The sound mixer said, "Speed," meaning his tape was rolling. The sound man was down below. The only microphone topside was a directional mike attached to the camera.

The cameraman clacked the slate in front of the lens. "Two-twenty-three double Papa, take one."

"And, action!" Peter cried.

George took a deep breath and blew it out. He pulled the lever to the right and the construction elevator rose to the top. He slowed it slightly, and stopped it level with the floor as Kenny had showed him.

George pulled the door open and stepped out.

A breeze was blowing. He hadn't noticed it before. He wondered if it had been there.

George moved out on the platform.

Teddy jumped down from the elevator.

George heard the sound and turned. He saw Teddy. Glanced around. There was no place to go.

George ran to the girder on the right. He stepped out on it and kept going.

Teddy followed. It was slightly windy, but he had no problem keeping his balance. He hoped George was all right. He hit his mark at ten feet. He stopped, looked down, and decided he wasn't going any farther. He raised his gun at George's back and fired.

The sound of the blank was loud.

The bullet presumably whistled past George's head.

George kept going.

Teddy fired again.

And missed.

He fired again.

George ducked into the 180-degree spin move. It was perfect. He aimed the Sig Sauer straight at Teddy and fired.

The bullet glanced off Teddy's ribs and knocked him backward off the beam, blood streaming from the blood bag and the wound. He fell in an awkward, helter-skelter heap.

Teddy knew he'd been shot. The thought raced through his mind, What a great take this is going to be for Peter.

Then everything went black.

81

T eddy came to in a hospital bed. He was vaguely aware of where he was. He blinked and tried to focus. There were a zillion tubes attached to him dripping fluids in and out. They restricted his movement, not that he was going anywhere. He hurt all over, a muted, dull pain. He figured one of the drips must be morphine. His pain was localized in his left leg, his head, and his chest. Just as he'd envisioned, the sniper had blown him off the beam. He should have trusted his instinct. Well, next time.

Tessa's face appeared through the haze. "You're awake! Thank God!"

"What are you doing here?"

"I was worried about you."

"Why aren't you on the set?"

"I'm done. Peter's shooting your scenes now."

"What?"

"When Peter found out you were going to make it, he called the stunt double, and he's shooting him."

"Is it working?"

"It's working fine. Peter caught your fall on film—it was perfect, by the way—and so all he needs to shoot is the low beam. Peter knows camera angles, and he's doing it with a stunt double."

"Does he need me to shoot close-ups?"

"You couldn't, even if he wanted you to. Your leg is broken, you were shot, and you have a concussion. Your head is wrapped in bandages. You look like a mummy."

Teddy reached up and felt the bandage.

Tessa shook her head. "I begged you to use a double for the stunt."

A nurse bustled in. "Well, well, look who joined the party. All right, miss. You've seen he's alive, and the doctor's coming. Don't get me in trouble now."

Tessa went out. Teddy closed his eyes. When he opened them again the doctor was examining him.

"Ah, there we are," the doctor said. "How are you feeling?"

"I thought you were supposed to tell me."

"My pleasure. You have a concussion, a broken leg, and a cracked rib from where the bullet grazed your side. The good news is your leg was not broken clean through. You have a fractured fibula. I operated and put a pin in it. Stay off it for three months and you'll be good as new. They'll teach you how to use the crutches in physical therapy."

"When can I get out of here?"

"Oh, sometime next week."

"That won't do."

"It will have to. You have a concussion. We have to monitor you to see if you're impaired."

"Give me a test."

"That's not how it works."

"Then get me out of the damn mummy costume and check out my head. I bet the swelling's gone down, or whatever the hell else is bothering you."

"Leave your bandages on or I'll put you in ICU. It was a fifty-fifty call whether you went there to begin with."

Teddy sank back in the bed in helpless frustration.

82

Mason Kimble and Gerard Cardigan watched the coverage on TV. Several spectators had caught Mark Weldon's fall on video, and all the news outlets were running them.

"Well," Gerard said, "it appears someone hates Ben Bacchetti as much as you do."

"Did the movie stop filming?"

"Not according to the *Hollywood Reporter*. Peter Barrington went ahead and filmed the rest of the scene with a stunt double."

"Resourceful boy. You think we should keep him on?"

Gerard laughed. "Yeah, right. As if he'd work for us."

"As if we'd want him," Mason said. "So who did this?"

"I have no idea."

"Clearly someone obsessed with the picture. First they burn the producer's house down, then they sabotage filming."

"Barnett wasn't working on this film," Gerard pointed out.

"So not the film. The studio. Someone was trying to fuck up the studio."

"Yes," Gerard said. "I don't know why, but I wish him Godspeed. By the time of the stockholders' meeting, they'll be eager to sell."

Mason looked at him sharply. "Are you *sure* you're not orchestrating this?"

"Would I lie to you?"

"How could I possibly know? You're so good at what you do, how could anyone possibly know?"

"It wasn't me."

"Really? Because it sounds like you. It's brilliant. It's elaborate. It gives us several degrees of separation, so much so that I don't even know if we did it."

"I take your point."

"If it's not you, who the hell is it?"

"Damned if I know."

83

Marsha Quickly wasn't happy. She'd been doing so well, and just like that it had all gone south. The pit boss blamed her for losing the high roller. She'd been out on the town, living the high life, drinking champagne, and right in the middle of the meal the guy got up to go to the bathroom and never came back.

It had taken her a while to realize it. She sat there at her table, sipping her drink and feeling like a queen, till finally, even in her tipsy state, she noticed that the gentleman had been gone an awfully long while. Now, how was that her fault?

As far as the pit boss was concerned, it was an unpardonable sin, and whether she was too standoffish or whether she'd had too much to drink, or whether she'd actually slapped the guy's face for being fresh, it didn't matter. He'd entrusted her with a precious jewel, and she'd tossed it away.

Immediately after that she found herself demoted. Not officially, she just started getting assigned the worst shifts, the worst tables. In short, she was working longer hours for less money. And there was no way of getting off the shit list. She couldn't appeal to Pete Genaro. Pete never bothered with the bar girls, except to cop a feel, and he wasn't going to offend his pit boss, not with everybody defecting to Sammy Candelosi.

Ginger, one of the girls she worked with, mentioned she was going to check out the rival casino. Marsha's loyalty to Pete Genaro extended only so far, and that was as far as it benefited her—there was no point in staying without the plum shifts. And rumor had it that Genaro wasn't going to be running the place for much longer anyway. If Pete was going down, Marsha wanted out from under him.

When Marsha got off her shift, instead of changing and going home, she slipped out quietly in her bar girl uniform and made her way next door to the Promised Land, Sammy Candelosi's casino.

She came in and walked the floor, hoping to see a pit boss she knew or a bar girl who'd give her a tip. Of course, she saw no one.

And then, miracle of miracles, there was Sammy Candelosi himself, weaving his way through the slot machines and out onto the floor. What a stroke of luck. A chance to impress him as an attractive woman with a winning personality.

Marsha was working her way across the floor in his direction when she noticed the man with him.

Her mouth fell open. She grabbed a passing bar girl with a

tray of empties. "Hey, sister, do me a favor. Who's that guy with Sammy Candelosi?"

The bar girl chuckled. "Him? Scary son of a bitch, isn't he? I'd stay away from him. That's Slythe, Sammy Candelosi's personal bodyguard."

84

Teddy was lucky the doctor had made him leave his head bandaged. The homicide cop was Sergeant O'Reilly. Teddy wondered how he was doing on the Ace Vargas case. Of course, he couldn't ask.

"This is a first for me," O'Reilly said. "I must say, I've never had someone shot on a five-story-high construction girder before."

"Did you figure out where the sniper was hiding?"

"Sniper? Mr. Weldon, there was no sniper. You were shot at point-blank range by the stuntman on the beam."

"What?"

"Yes. George Perkins. He's been questioned thoroughly, and it appears he was an unwitting accomplice. He fired a gun he thought contained blanks. The perpetrator appears to be a man who gave his name as Tim Dale and posed as a weapons expert. We'd like to question him as a suspect, but he slipped away during the confusion after your fall. But there is some rather strong corroborating evidence. The man whose place he took, prop man Fred Russell, was found dead in his foyer with his throat cut. The man posing as Tim Dale took his place."

Teddy frowned.

"Did you ever get a good look at him?"

"Frankly, no. There were too many other things going on. And he was always peripheral. Jackson rigged me with the squib, and he just checked it. Jackson is probably the one who had the most contact with him."

"He's been questioned, but he wasn't very helpful. He basically described the baseball cap the man was wearing."

"Too bad."

"You're lucky the fall didn't kill you. This guy slashed your landing balloon so it deflated on impact."

Teddy frowned again.

"Now then," Sergeant O'Reilly said, "that is an awful lot of work to kill one person. Can you think of anyone who would want you dead that badly?"

"It makes no sense to me," Teddy said. "I'm a bit player. Now, Brad Hunter is another story. He's a star, and a more likely target for some nut job. Or maybe someone just wanted to stop filming to harm the picture, or the studio."

"You're working awfully hard to convince me that the target wasn't you."

"Because it makes no sense. It's flattering, but I just can't see it."

"Are you up to looking at some pictures?"

"Do you have them?"

"We're putting them together. We'll run them through this

prop man first, but, like I say, he's not very observant. Do you think you'd know the man if you saw him again?"

"It's possible, but if the guy's any good, he won't look anything like the man I saw. And he has to be good to pull off a bluff like that. He shouldn't have even been able to get on the lot."

"I know. The guard is taking a bit of heat, and so is the head of the props department for not checking him out with the union."

"Of course, in hindsight you know to do that. In the normal course of events when you're making a picture, it's rush, rush, rush, and if something goes wrong you deal with the practical part of the problem instead of the official details. It's an emergency, can the guy do the job, if so who cares where he came from."

"Can you think of anything else that could help us?"

"Not a thing."

"Okay," O'Reilly said. "Just hang in there. I'll be back."

"Don't rush."

S lythe didn't like to leave things half done. The initial report that stuntman Mark Weldon had been critically injured in a fall on a movie set had been satisfactory enough to send him back to Las Vegas with the feeling of accomplishment.

When further reports from the hospital indicated that while Mark Weldon's leg was indeed broken, he was not in critical condition and was expected to make a full recovery, Slythe headed back to L.A.

85

The nurse had just gone out after taking Teddy's vitals when the phone rang in his room.

He scooped it up. "Yes?"

"Billy?"

"I'm afraid you have the wrong number."

"I'm sorry. It's me, Marsha Quickly. I'm an actress. I worked with you on the film."

"Oh?"

"Just one scene, it's not important. But I knew you from before. My name is Bambi, I was a friend of Charmaine's. I work for Pete Genaro at the New Desert Inn and Casino."

"Give me a reason not to hang up the phone."

"I heard what happened to you and I'm afraid it might be my fault. I'm back in Vegas, working for Pete like I said, and I told him I saw you. He's in the middle of a casino war with a mobster out of New Jersey named Sammy Candelosi. I mentioned you'd be just the guy to handle that."

"Oh, you did, did you?"

"Hey, I didn't mean anything by it. We were just shooting the shit. Anyway, I think Sammy Candelosi heard somehow that I mentioned your name. At least that's how I dope it out, because of what happened."

"What happened?"

"After your house burned down and you escaped, everyone wanted to know where producer Billy Barnett was, only to be told he's on vacation and can't be reached. And that made a lot of people very nervous.

"The next thing I know this high roller is taking me out to dinner and plying me with wine and drinks, and before the son of a bitch ran out on me, he started talking about motion pictures, asking what work I've done lately, and somehow or other the conversation got around to me running into you on the set of that movie, and before the guy took off I think I may have mentioned you were working under the name Mark Weldon."

"Oh, did you now?" Teddy said with wry irritation.

"Yeah, but that's not the worst of it."

"What happened?"

"I just found out the high roller who took me out is a hit man for Sammy Candelosi."

86

lythe had no problem finding the room. Billy Barnett was checked into the hospital under the name Mark Weldon, and the nurse at admitting was very helpful. She told Slythe that he had no visitors, but she looked up his room number to find that out, and she made no secret of it. Mark Weldon was in room 608.

Slythe went out, walked around the hospital, and came in another entrance. He walked up to the desk and said, "Outpatient surgery?"

"Third floor."

Slythe nodded his thanks and walked onto the elevator. He didn't get off on three, however, but went up to six and located the patients' wing. He walked down the hall toward 608, looking for an unlocked supply closet. He found one right off the bat. He slipped in, closed the door, and locked it.

He couldn't find a doctor's coat, but there were sets of scrubs folded on a shelf. He shrugged off his clothes, stashed them behind a hamper in the corner, and put on some scrubs.

He looked around and found a surgical cap. He put it on and tucked his hair into it. It wouldn't fool Billy Barnett, who would no doubt recognize him as the phony prop man, but it should work on anyone else.

He grabbed a clipboard as a useful prop. Somehow it made him feel more official.

He didn't bother looking for a scalpel. He had his razor. He retrieved it from his pile of clothes and slid it into the pants pocket of his scrubs.

He peeked out the door to make sure no one was coming, and slipped out into the hallway.

T eddy got off the phone, thinking hard. He had to reassess the situation. What Marsha had told him completely changed the game. A guy—a mobster—named Sammy Candelosi thought Pete Genaro had hired Teddy to take him out.

That was just what Teddy was looking for: someone else with a reason to kill him.

So Sammy Candelosi knew Pete Genaro had called him, but not from Marsha. Candelosi's goon had pumped her for information because he already knew Genaro had tried to hire him. Which meant Pete Genaro had a leak in his organization. It didn't matter who it was. As long as there was a traitor, Teddy could exploit it for his own purposes. Which included taking out Sammy Candelosi. Ironically, by trying to eliminate a threat, Sammy Candelosi had merely activated one.

The pieces were falling into place. The fire could have been set by anyone, but the attack at the construction site had been

Sammy Candelosi's doing. It was carried out by someone who knew that Billy Barnett and Mark Weldon were one and the same person. Sammy Candelosi had just learned that.

Teddy sucked in his breath. That brought up another real possibility. Sammy Candelosi had tried to kill Mark Weldon because he found out Mark Weldon was Billy Barnett. Sammy believed Billy Barnett had been hired to kill him, and would have even more reason to do it now. And Teddy was checked into the hospital under the name Mark Weldon. There was nothing to stop Sammy Candelosi from having him killed in his bed as he lay there helplessly with his leg in traction.

Teddy needed a gun. He didn't want to alarm Peter, but he didn't want to die in his bed either. The thing was, aside from the Barringtons and the Bacchettis, Teddy was hard-pressed to think of anyone who knew the situation and could provide him with one.

The answer was Mike Freeman. Teddy hated to bother him without being able to produce Nigel Hightower, but this was a special situation. Teddy reached for the phone.

The door opened and a man in scrubs with a clipboard came in. Even in his drugged state, Teddy was suddenly on high alert. There was nothing he could put his finger on, but from his years of experience at the CIA, Teddy knew instinctively that something was wrong. This man was not a doctor.

Teddy braced himself for the attack.

The man had the upper hand, but Teddy had the element of surprise. The hit man wouldn't be expecting any resistance. Not from a cripple in bed who had no idea an attack was coming.

The man in scrubs set down the clipboard and approached the bed.

Teddy had his hand on the bedpan. It was unused, but it was under the sheets. The nurse had left it there so he would have easy access. Under the cover of the sheet, he slid it off the bed so that it hung down the side, firmly gripped in his left hand.

The man stepped back and smiled. "You planning to hit me with that bedpan? I'd rather you didn't. Mike Freeman sent me. Peter Barrington's concerned for your safety and hired Strategic Services for security. If someone wants to kill you, they'll have to go through me."

Teddy grinned and handed him the bedpan. "You want to set this over there? I'm tired of looking at the damn thing."

87

ike Freeman's agent's name was Rick. He was a good
man, but a little too by-the-book for Teddy's taste. He
would not approve of what Teddy was about to do.

Teddy sent him to change out of his scrubs and
back into his suit, and station himself outside the door—he'd
be of more use there where he could intimidate troublemakers,
rather than in the room pretending to be a doctor anyway.

As soon as Rick was gone, Teddy picked up the phone and
called Mike Freeman. "Mike?"

"Yes."

"Thanks for your man. I only just realized there might be a
need myself."

"Don't thank me. It was Peter's idea."

"So I understand. You didn't mention to him our previous
employment?"

"I'm insulted you have to ask."

"Hey, my leg's in traction and I'm doped up on painkillers. I
see potential dangers everywhere."

"Well, you can stop worrying. I've got men on you around the clock until Peter tells me to stop. When he does, I'll check with you before I pull my team, just so you'll know."

"From you I would expect no less. Listen, I'm in a bit of a situation here, and I'm going to need to get myself out."

"How can I help?"

"I don't want to shock your man, and I don't want to get into an argument with him either. I need to do what I need to do, and I don't need a well-meaning agent wrestling me back into bed. I need him to do what I tell him without checking with you, even if what I'm doing may seem a trifle unorthodox."

"I'll read him the riot act."

"Want me to put him on the phone? He's right outside the door."

"That won't work. My men are well trained. I'll call him from my phone so he knows for certain it's me."

Teddy got off the phone. Almost immediately he heard his bodyguard's cell phone ring in the hall. Mike Freeman would be explaining the facts of life. The agent might not like it, but he'd have to go along. Teddy would be free to put his plan in motion.

He just needed a plan.

Slythe was hiding out in a stall in the men's room. He'd gotten to room 608 only to find another man in scrubs standing by the bed. He'd walked right on by and searched the floor until he found a men's room where he could hole up and wait.

He waited ten minutes, then came out of the stall and retraced his steps to the room.

Now a man in a suit and tie was sitting in a chair outside the door, either a plainclothes cop or a hired security guard. Whichever he was, he put the kibosh on Slythe's plan. The risks of taking out a guard were just too great. He'd give up for now—Barnett was no threat to anyone at the moment.

He kept walking and ducked into the supply closet again. He took his razor out of the pocket, pulled off his scrubs, and added them to the pile in the hamper. He dressed quickly and left.

A nurse caught him coming out the door. "Hey. You're not allowed in there."

Slythe grinned sheepishly. "Sorry, I thought it was the men's room," he said, and walked off.

The nurse didn't press the issue. Slythe took the elevator down to the lobby, left the hospital, and hailed a cab to the airport.

88

eddy called Herbie Fisher at Woodman & Weld. He waited until he was alone to do it. Aside from not wanting anyone to overhear the conversation, Herbie knew him as Billy Barnett, not Mark Weldon, and it was Weldon who was checked into the hospital.

Once a protégé of Stone Barrington, Herbie was now a senior partner at Woodman & Weld, and one of their most respected lawyers. Though he usually handled major cases, Herbie could always be counted on to do legal favors for friends.

Herbie was glad to hear from him. "Billy, what's up? I hear you're making a movie."

"Boy, are you behind on the news."

Teddy caught him up on the situation with Sammy Candelosi and Pete Genaro, and how he'd ended up in the hospital. It seemed urgent enough, even leaving out Tessa's problems and the whole corporate takeover.

Herbie was shocked. "Someone tried to kill you? That's terrible. Is there anything I can do?"

"Get me out of here."

———

Teddy's doctor was horrified. "You can't check out."

"Actually, I can," Teddy said. "I just have to sign a waiver that I am checking out against medical advice. Then the hospital's covered, and they're happy to get the bed. I have an attorney standing by, if you need it explained to you."

"Your leg's in traction."

"Only because you put it there. Take it out of traction, and I'll be on my way."

"I'm not going to do that."

"It's all right, I will." Teddy unhooked the cable holding up his leg. "Ta-da! Now, if you'll just have a nurse bring a wheelchair, I'm good to go."

It wasn't quite as easy as that, but at least Teddy didn't have to resort to a legal injunction. Two hours later a nurse wheeled him out the emergency room exit where Rick was waiting with a car.

Teddy slid into the backseat, and Rick took off.

"Did you get the items I requested?"

Rick jerked his thumb. "It's all in the trunk. Scalpel, surgical scissors, surgical saw, needle and surgical thread, Ace bandages, adhesive tape, antibiotic ointment, a pair of crutches, and a wheelchair."

"No cookies?"

"I could arrange for a grocery delivery. You're not getting shot while I'm shopping."

"I was kidding."

"Oh," Rick said. Clearly joking about such a serious subject was not in his nature.

The super at Mark Weldon's apartment building was out front when Rick pulled up. He raised his eyebrows when Teddy emerged on crutches. "Whoa. What happened to you?"

"I had an accident on the set."

His eyes widened. "Are you the stuntman who fell?"

"My fame precedes me."

"No, really. You fell from the fifth floor?"

"The fall was what we were filming. There was a landing pad staged below."

"Looks like you missed."

"This is nothing," Teddy said, referring to the crutches. "Tomorrow I'll be back on the set."

The super looked doubtful.

Rick helped Teddy up the stairs to his apartment. "You want me to leave the wheelchair in the car?" Rick asked. "It's going to be a bitch getting it up and down the stairs."

"I'm going to leave you in the car, too," Teddy said. "Park down the street where you can watch the door. Call me on the phone if you see anyone suspicious trying to get in."

"I could sit by the door."

"You're not an aide, you're a bodyguard. You can't sit outside the door, and inside you'll drive me nuts. Go set up a good surveillance point. I'll call you if I need anything."

That wasn't the way Rick would have played it, but Mike's instructions had been explicit.

As soon as Rick was gone, Teddy locked the door behind him. He took out his gun and set it on the table for easy access.

Then he got down to work.

89

Teddy couldn't have a cast on for what he intended to do. He took the cast off and examined the leg. The doctor had done a good job of setting it. With the cast on, it would heal rather quickly. With the cast off, it would be all right if he didn't put any pressure on it.

Teddy had to put pressure on it.

Teddy covered the wound with sterile pads, and wrapped them in adhesive tape. He bracketed the broken area with wooden splints. They wouldn't hold as well as the cast, but they would be better than nothing. He taped them tight, making the splint as thin as possible.

He wrapped the leg in Ace bandages, so tight as to cut off the circulation. He was risking gangrene, but it couldn't be helped. He had two criteria: he couldn't stagger, and he couldn't fall down.

Teddy pulled on a pair of suit pants. The bottom of the leg looked slightly bulky, but it would have to do.

Teddy limped into the bathroom and looked at his face in

the mirror. It was shocking. His mummy costume was so extensive he could have passed for the Invisible Man. As in that movie, he could imagine unwinding the bandage and finding nothing there.

Teddy cut through the bandage with surgical scissors. It unwound easily, a good sign. His face wasn't bad. He had a few cuts and bruises, but nothing that makeup wouldn't hide. His forehead was still gashed and swollen, but it was near the hairline where it could be covered with a wig.

And he wasn't suffering the effects of a concussion. He staggered a little when he let go of the sink, but that wasn't from dizziness, that was from the broken leg.

He was good to go.

In his long years of equipping CIA operatives for missions, Teddy had drilled one idea into their heads: It is inadvisable to meet the same person under two separate identities. No matter how good you are, or think you are, there is always something that will trip you up. Some small characteristic that you don't even realize you have, but which triggers a flash of doubt in the person you are attempting to fool. It is far better to send a second agent, even one not as proficient as you might think you are.

Teddy was not one to disregard his own advice, but he had no other agent, and he needed to call on Mason Kimble and Gerard Cardigan again. He had met them as a dirty old man, eager to hang out with movie types. He needed to get as far away from that image as possible, particularly as his pitch this time would be the same—a desire to invest in movies. To pull it off, Teddy went younger and Italian. Carlo Verdi had thick black hair threatening to creep down his face as sideburns. He put on a flashy suit, and transformed himself into a New Jersey wiseguy.

Once again, Teddy had no problem getting into Star Pictures. They had no secretary, so they had to answer the door.

Gerard Cardigan opened it.

"Mason Kimble?" Teddy said.

"Gerard Cardigan. How can we help you?"

Teddy jerked his thumb in Mason's direction. "That Mr. Kimble?" He stepped around Gerard, grabbed Mason's hand, and pumped it up and down. "Mr. Kimble, Carlo Verdi. I'm here on behalf of Sammy Candelosi." When Mason showed no sign of recognition, Teddy frowned and said, "You are familiar with Sammy Candelosi?"

Mason and Gerard looked at each other.

"No, we are not," Mason said.

"Well, I won't tell him. He might take it as a slight. It is not wise to offend Sammy Candelosi. Particularly when you are thinking of becoming his partner."

Mason and Gerard looked at each other again.

"Excuse me," Mason said. "What gave you the idea we are thinking of making Sammy Candelosi our partner?"

"The fact that you took this meeting."

"We took this meeting because you walked in off the street and demanded it."

"My point exactly. If Sammy Candelosi wants something, he gets it. He wanted this meeting, therefore he got it. In the future, you will find it better not to second-guess Sammy, but to figure out what he wants and go along with that."

"Now, see here—" Mason said.

Carlo Verdi put up his hand. "You're offended. It was not my intention to give offense. It would be very unfortunate for all involved, and for the two of you in particular. Please understand Sammy is not trying to muscle in here. Sammy is not trying to take over your business. Sammy is not trying to push you around. Sammy merely wishes to make money. He is a businessman. Making money is first and foremost his goal.

"*Keeping* money is his second goal. That is where so many people fall down. They make money, and, poof, it is gone. That is particularly true of a person involved in the casino business, as Sammy Candelosi happens to be. That is why he would like to diversify. He would like to take some of his money out of gambling and invest it in motion pictures."

Mason blinked. "He wants to invest in our movies?"

"I thought I made that clear. It so happens that Sammy needs to invest a certain amount of his money in a legitimate business venture. Motion pictures is not only legitimate, it is a volatile industry with potential losses and gains in the millions. Our bookkeeper would love to have a look."

Gerard stuck his chin forward. "Why us? This is a town with hundreds of movie companies. What makes ours attractive?"

"As Star Pictures, you're not. But it has come to Sammy's attention that there is an excellent chance Star Pictures will be merging with a major studio in the near future."

"Where did you hear that?" Gerard said.

"Sammy hears everything. If you don't want Sammy to hear something, don't do it."

"What did Sammy hear?"

"Sammy heard Centurion Studios might be ripe for the taking. Under the circumstances, your production company might seem like a good investment, particularly if one were to get in on the ground floor.

"At any rate, Sammy would like to make you a proposal. He would like to make it to you in person. He will not come to you. You will come to him. Sammy will be happy to comp you at his casino, but he will have no contact with you there, as he is not eager to let the details of his business affairs leak out. He will meet you at a restaurant of his own choosing, away from the hotel, with a private room where you can talk business."

Mason and Gerard looked at each other.

Mason said, "Just for the sake of argument, how much is Sammy considering investing?"

Teddy shrugged and spread his hands. "Over a long period of time, we're talking a considerable amount of money. But as an initial investment, somewhere in the neighborhood of one hundred million dollars."

Mason Kimble managed not to seem too eager. It took an effort.

He nodded. "That's something we could consider."

90

Teddy took a taxi back to his apartment. The cell phone rang on his way up the walk. He managed not to react until he was safely in the front door, out of sight of Mike Freeman's agent. He pulled the phone out of his pocket. "Yeah?"

"A man in a cab just pulled up in front of the building. He looks like he could have mob connections."

"You ever see him before?"

"Yes. He came out of your building about an hour ago."

"Curly dark hair, sideburns, cheap-looking suit?"

"That's him."

"It's okay. He lives here. Thanks for the heads-up."

Teddy limped up the stairs to his apartment and collapsed on the bed. He allowed himself five minutes to catch his breath. Then he sat up, pulled off his Carlo Verdi wig, and stripped off his wiseguy clothes.

His leg didn't look as bad as it felt. There was nothing to

indicate it was anything worse than a bad sprain. Bad enough to require three Ace bandages, but even so.

Teddy unwound the Ace bandages and took off the splint. As expected, blood had seeped through the adhesive-taped bandage underneath. Teddy cut it off with surgical scissors.

The wound was ugly. He cleaned it up and rebandaged it. He put the splint back on and taped it tight. It hurt like hell. The doctor had given him painkillers, but he hadn't taken them. He needed to be alert, even if all he was going to do was sleep. Mike Freeman's men were good, but they weren't infallible. Still, he was glad to have one there.

Teddy flung himself down on the bed and was almost instantly asleep.

A t seven in the morning Teddy woke. First order of business was to check the wound. It hadn't seeped much during the night. He changed the bandage again and rebound the leg.

Then he put the cast back on. That was harder. He taped it up on the open side and reinforced it with surgical thread.

Teddy called Sammy Candelosi's hotel and casino and gave the name Carlo Verdi. He'd been careful to use an alias for whom he had credit cards. "I'd like to book a two-bedroom suite under the name Mason Kimble and Gerard Cardigan. Their expenses are being comped, including chips if they wish to gamble. If they try to pay for anything, tell them it's been taken care of."

"Yes, Mr. Verdi."

"I'm not sure if they're checking in tonight or tomorrow, but book the room starting today."

"Yes, of course."

Teddy hung up and finished working on his cast. It didn't look bad. He tried walking on his crutches with it. It didn't fall off, which was all he'd hoped for. It wasn't doing a thing to support his leg.

He got a pair of pants from the closet, took the surgical scissors, and slit the outside of the left leg from the cuff all the way up well past the knee. He sat on the edge of the bed and pulled the pants on over the cast. They fit fine, and hid the slit in the cast, which was on the inside of the leg. He now looked like exactly what he was: an orthopedic patient with a broken leg.

Teddy transformed himself back into Billy Barnett. He put on a clean shirt, and the jacket that went with the pants. He put on his right shoe and sock. His left foot he left bare.

Teddy unlocked the padlock on his closet and took out some equipment, mostly small and portable due to his situation. He chose a couple of handguns, a shoulder holster, a few IDs, credentials and credit cards, and a small makeup kit to approximate the ones chosen. He put them all in an inconspicuous bag such as a tradesman might carry.

As an afterthought, he threw in the Ace Vargas gun that had been sent to Tessa. With luck, he might have use for it.

When he was done, he locked the closet. He took another small bag, filled it with medical equipment, and added clean socks, underwear, and toiletries.

When he was ready he requested an Uber. The app told him a cab was five minutes away.

Teddy got on the crutches and managed to balance the bags. He gritted his teeth and hobbled to the door.

Paco came out of his apartment. He was startled to see another man on crutches coming down the stairs.

"You the super here?" Teddy said, cutting off any inquiry. "I'm in hospital rehab services. We coach first-time orthopedic fracture patients. Your stairs are not up to safety standards. I could have fallen. I don't want to write you up. If you could just put in a handrail, I'm sure the patient would appreciate it. I'll pretend I didn't see this, but I'm going to be back on Monday, if you know what I mean. Would you mind getting the door?"

The super bought it. He not only got the door, he carried Teddy's bags out to the cab.

Teddy had the cab drive around the block and drop him off at his car, which was parked out of sight from the super. He gave the confused driver fifty bucks for the incredibly short ride and rated him five stars.

The grateful driver happily put his bags in the car for him.

Teddy's phone rang as he drove off.

"Hello?"

"Mark, it's Rick. I thought you should know that another man on crutches just came out of your building. He didn't look like Mark Weldon, but he's the spitting image of Billy Barnett, and I happen to know Mike Freeman would want me to follow Billy Barnett."

"Where are you?"

"Look in the rearview mirror."

Teddy did. Rick was right behind him.

"Good man. Listen, Rick. Give Mike a call. Tell him I'm

leaving town and I won't need his services until I come back, which means you can knock off as of now. First, drop back and make sure no one else is following me. If you can't spot a tail in the next ten miles, you're off the clock."

"Are you sure?"

"Call Mike. He'll tell you. By the way, you did a good job, and I'll be sure to let him know," Teddy said, and hung up.

91

The pilot was shocked to see Teddy on crutches. "Mr. Barnett, what happened to you?"

Teddy grinned sheepishly. "Slipped in the shower. Totally embarrassing. I was on the floor naked when the EMTs got there."

"Do you want to use the apartment to convalesce?"

"No, but I'd like to use my plane. I assume it's set to fly?"

"You can fly a plane like that?"

"Why not? I don't use my left leg much."

"This must have just happened. Aren't you on pain medication?"

"Not so you could notice. The doctor prescribed them, but that doesn't mean I have to take them. Stiff upper lip and all that."

"I can't send someone up in your condition."

"You're not sending anyone up. You don't run the airport. You manage a hangar. You do it very well, but you don't control the air."

"Peter's going to want to know why I let you go up."

"Peter's making a movie. I'll be back before he's done."

The pilot sighed. "All right. Do you need any help?"

"You can roll it out for me and throw my bags in."

The pilot stowed Teddy's bags in the plane and tugged it out the bay door. He watched as Teddy hobbled up to it on crutches.

"I'd feel better if you let me go with you," he said.

"I know, but I need you here." Teddy smiled. "Thanks for the launch."

Teddy climbed into the pilot's seat and checked the dials. He hadn't flown in a while, except for his trip with Nigel Hightower III. It didn't matter. A night's sleep had done him a world of good. The drugs were wearing off, and he was thinking clearly. And flying was second nature to him.

He laid in a course for Las Vegas and took off.

I n Vegas Teddy set down and taxied to a private hangar. The pilot in charge was surprised to see a man on crutches climb out of the cockpit. But when Teddy presented two crisp hundred-dollar bills, he gamely removed Teddy's bags and helped him to a cab without comment. He understood about things that happen in Vegas.

Teddy told him, "I'll be leaving the plane for a day or two, maybe three."

"You got it," the pilot said with a grin.

Teddy took his cab straight to the New Desert Inn and Casino.

He was not surprised to find a curvy secretary seated at the

desk outside Pete Genaro's office. He smiled. Pete's taste in fe-
male employees would never change.

"May I help you?" she said.

"Pete Genaro."

She picked up the phone. "Who shall I say is calling?"

Teddy walked toward the closed office door. "It's too complicated. I'll just tell him."

"You can't go in there."

"It's all right. He'll be glad to see me."

Teddy pushed the door open with one crutch and hobbled in.

Pete Genaro was seated at his desk, about to light a cigar. It
fell from his hands when he saw Teddy.

"Hi, Pete. How's it going?"

Teddy and Pete were seated in chairs with brandies. Teddy
didn't need a brandy, but he saw no reason not to be social.

"When you first asked me for help, I wasn't in a position to
assist. Times have changed."

"I see. Now that your service isn't so valuable, you're willing
to give it."

"Granted, I am not in the best physical condition. What you
see is what you get."

"What changed your mind?"

"For one thing, Sammy Candelosi burned down my house, a
bad move on his part, and it's coming back to bite him. I may
not be a hundred percent, but I can still handle the likes of him.
Which of your men knows the most about him?"

"That would be Jake, my personal bodyguard. I have him spying on their operation."

"Get him in here. I have a lot of ground to cover, and I'd hate to do it twice."

Genaro snatched up the phone. "Sherry, get Jake in here."

"I don't know where he is," she protested.

"He's got a cell phone, doesn't he? Get him in here." Pete hung up and shook his head. "I swear, if she wasn't so darn pretty."

Jake showed up fifteen minutes later. He gawked at the man with the cast on his leg.

"Don't look so surprised, Jake," Pete said. "This is Billy Barnett, the man Bambi advised me to call."

"Let me fill you in," Teddy said. "Pete called me to help with a mobster named Sammy Candelosi. At the time, I was not eager to do it, but certain things have changed. He burned down my house. Now I've purchased a new one and I'm getting it renovated, but before I move in I need to be sure it won't burn down, too. That's where you can help. You have the inside track with Sammy Candelosi. Pete tells me you know more about his operation than anyone else. You can tell me what I need to know. First off, how many bodyguards does he travel with?"

"Just one, but the guy's a stone-cold killer. Scares the shit out of me. Guy named Slythe. Tall, thin, long hair, carries a straight razor. Candelosi's got other goons, but that's the one he's always with."

"How many other goons does he have?"

"Hard to say. They're scattered throughout the casino. Some

are goons, some are bouncers, some are pit bosses. Most of them are local. He's got maybe ten or twelve men he brought from Jersey."

"Suppose he went out to dinner. Not at his casino, but at a private dining room at a restaurant in town. How many men would he take?"

"It would depend on who he's dining with. If he were on a hot date, there wouldn't be many and she wouldn't see them."

"Say it was a business meeting with a couple of out-of-town guys that he didn't know."

"He'd bring muscle. Slythe for sure, maybe five or six others."

Teddy nodded. He turned to Pete. "Okay, here's the pitch. I said I'd handle this for you, but obviously I can't. I do owe you for the Russian, and I like what you said on the phone. I can't do it myself, but I need to get it done. So I lined up two guys to do the job. They're young, but they're good. They're protégés of mine, actually, and they owe me, just like I owe you. I'm not going to give you their names—in fact, you're not going to meet them. They're going to contact Sammy Candelosi posing as young movie executives with their own studio in Hollywood, who want to talk to him about a multimillion-dollar money-laundering scheme. They're going to set up a dinner meeting with him in a private dining room at an out-of-town restaurant. That's why I want to know how many goons he'll have with him."

Teddy turned back to Jake. "So I want you to keep an eye on him. When he agrees to the dinner, I want to know it, and I want to know how many goons he's going to bring. Can you do that?"

Jake looked at Pete.

Pete nodded. "What Billy tells you, consider it comes from me."

"Yeah, I can do it."

"Good man," Teddy said. "Go see what you can find."

When Jake went out, Pete said, "You're paying these guys yourself?"

"They're doing me a favor."

"You always were a stand-up guy."

Teddy jerked his thumb in the direction Jake had gone. "You think he can do it?"

"He's not very bright. I think that's why Sammy lets him hang around. He's no real threat."

"No argument here."

Pete frowned. "Why did you ask him to report in when Sammy agrees to the dinner? Won't your hit men do that?"

"Yes, they will," Teddy said.

"Then why did you ask him?"

Teddy smiled. "To see if he does."

Pete raised his brandy snifter. "I always knew you were smart."

92

Jake burst into Sammy Candelosi's office. "Billy Barnett's here!"

Sammy frowned. "Are you sure?"

"Yeah, but don't worry," Jake said. "He's got a cast on his leg."

"Then why is he here?"

"He came to help Pete. Pete asked him to take you out. He can't do it, but he lined up two hit men to do it for him."

"Two hit men?"

"Yeah. They're going to call you up posing as movie types and ask you out to dinner to discuss a deal. They plan to hit you during dinner."

"Son of a bitch."

"But now you know not to go."

"Yeah." Sammy frowned.

"What's the matter?" Jake said.

"If we don't go, they'll just try something else," Slythe said.

"On the other hand, this gives us an excellent opportunity to neutralize the threat."

"When did you hear this?" Sammy said.

"Just now, in Pete's office. Barnett sent me here to see if you're going to go for it."

Sammy smiled grimly. "Oh, I'm going to go for it."

93

Pete Genaro comped Teddy the Presidential Suite with every extravagance imaginable, from the bar, pool table, and sauna to the balcony terrace with barbecue grill. Ordinarily Teddy had no use for such excesses, but he had had no chance to clean himself up since the hospital. The bathroom featured a walk-in marble shower with three-sixty jets and a wraparound marble bench.

Teddy had been told he couldn't get his cast wet, but the doctor hadn't planned on him taking it off. Teddy got in the shower, washed up, and cleaned his wounds. He had almost forgotten the one on his side, it was so minor compared to the rest. Ironic that getting shot was the least of his problems. He washed it off while he waited for the throbbing in his leg to subside.

When he was done, Teddy dried himself off, hobbled on crutches to the bed, and went to work with his medical kit. He bandaged the wound in his chest and taped up his leg. He wouldn't bother with the cast until he had to go out. It was decorative only.

Teddy took out one of the burner phones he'd brought along and called Mason Kimble at Star Pictures. "Mr. Kimble. This is Carlo Verdi. Sammy Candelosi would like to meet you and Mr. Cardigan for dinner tomorrow night. I'm arranging the details now. I've booked a high-roller two-bedroom suite for you and Mr. Cardigan. It's available now, but you can come tonight or tomorrow. I regret that we do not have our own private plane, but let me know what flight you are going to take and I will book you first class. Don't worry about transportation, you'll be met at the airport. Check in and enjoy the casino, all expenses are comped. Don't try to contact Sammy at the casino. I'll let you know when it's time. Does that work for you?"

"That will be just fine."

"Good." Teddy gave him the number of the burner phone. "Call me at this number when you decide what flight you want to take and I'll set it up."

Teddy figured he'd done a good day's work. He lay down on the bed and was almost instantly asleep.

94

We have to get there early," Gerard said.

"Why?" Mason said. "We're going first class."

"I need time to check in my gun."

"You don't need a gun. It's a business meeting."

"A business meeting with a mobster. I'm wearing a gun."

"He's an investor."

"He's an investor who happens to be a mobster."

"Are you saying we shouldn't go?"

"No, I'm just saying I'm taking my gun."

"You're taking a gun through the airport?"

"Why not? I have no police record because my heart is pure, and I'm very good at what I do. Trust me, there won't be a problem."

There wasn't. Fully paid first-class tickets were waiting for them at the airport. They only had to present IDs. Gerard checked his gun, and they were good to go.

They got off the plane in Vegas to find a chauffeur with the sign KIMBLE AND CARDIGAN waiting at baggage claim. He took them to the casino, carried their bags, and refused a tip.

"It's taken care of," he said.

The desk clerk was equally gracious. When Mason Kimble presented his driver's license and a credit card, he handed the credit card back. "Just the ID. Everything is taken care of. You just have to sign for it."

"This is wonderful," Mason said as the bellboy led them up to the room.

"It's too good to be true," Gerard said. "I don't like it."

"You worry too much," Mason said. "Can't you just enjoy it?"

"Sure," Gerard said, but he wasn't entirely happy.

It was almost reassuring when the bellboy accepted a tip.

95

Teddy spent the morning checking out restaurants. It wasn't easy on crutches, but he'd narrowed them down online. The first two were unacceptable, their private rooms *too* private for his needs.

The third one was the charm. The Golden Grill had exactly what he needed—a room on the ground floor with a table that could easily seat a dozen and a high window on the back wall. Teddy inquired as to its availability for a birthday party the following month, got prices, and told them he'd call.

He went back to his suite at the casino, called them up, and booked the room for six o'clock that night with Carlo Verdi's credit card.

When the room was booked he called Mason Kimble. He had his cell phone number, but first he tried him in the hotel suite.

Mason was in the hot tub, but of course there was a phone within reach. He picked it up. "Hello?"

"Mr. Kimble?"

"Yes."

"Carlo Verdi. Are your accommodations satisfactory?"

"Quite."

"I have dinner set for six o'clock tonight at the Golden Grill."

"Good. We'll be there."

He had one more call to make.

S ammy Candelosi had Slythe, Jake, and four goons in his office when the call came through. All were tough, all were
armed, all had come with him from Jersey.

"Yes?" Sammy said.

"Sammy Candelosi? This is Mason Kimble. Gerard Cardigan and I would be happy to meet you for dinner at the Golden
Grill at six o'clock tonight to discuss an arrangement I think
you will find financially advantageous."

"Who the hell are you?"

"We're movie producers, the owners of Star Pictures in
Hollywood."

Sammy looked over at Jake and nodded his head. "Movie producers. And you want to meet me tonight at the Golden Grill?"

"That's right. At six o'clock in their private dining room. Will
that work for you?"

Sammy glanced around at the men assembled in his office.
"Absolutely," he said, and hung up the phone.

"That's it," Jake said. "Those are the guys."

"They sure are," Sammy said. "And we've got time to pre-
pare a little surprise for them. Nice work, Jake."

"I gotta report back to Pete," Jake said. "Tell him you got the
call so he doesn't know you're wise."

96

Teddy packed his bags, called the bellboy, and tipped him handsomely to leave them outside where the valets summoned cabs. He'd gotten confirmation from Jake, via Pete, that the dinner was on, and it was time for him to play his part.

"Are you checking out, sir?"

"No, just going out for the afternoon, and I can't carry them very well."

"Do you want me to call you a cab?"

"No, it takes me a while to do things. Leave them with the valet and tell him I'll be down."

Teddy gave the bellboy five minutes to clear the lobby so the desk clerk wouldn't think he was checking out, took one last look around the suite, and went out the door. He was getting better on the crutches. He motored through the lobby and went out front where his bags were waiting with the head valet.

Teddy slipped him a fifty and said, "Thanks for watching my bags. I'll be needing a cab."

"Yes, sir. Where will you be wanting to go?"

"Several places. I'll negotiate with the driver."

"Yes, sir." He waved over a cab.

The cabbie loaded Teddy's bags and helped Teddy in. "Where to?"

"We'll be making a couple of stops."

"I have to put down a destination."

"The New Desert Inn and Casino."

"That's here."

"That's where we'll end up. It shouldn't take more than a few hours." Teddy handed him a couple of hundred-dollar bills. "If it does, you'll be well compensated."

"Sounds good." The driver picked up his car phone. "Where to first?"

"Must you call it in?"

"That's procedure."

"Here's the deal," Teddy said. "My wife has detectives on my tail. They're watching cabs and car services, so there's no reason to be specific. You've got a tourist on a sightseeing trip. Whatever your company wants to charge me is fine, but this is between us." Teddy slapped two more hundred-dollar bills in the cabbie's hand.

"Works for me," the cabbie said. "What unspecified location would you like to sightsee first?"

"Let's swing by the airport."

The cabbie took him out to the airport. Teddy called the pilot he'd left his plane with on the way. Then he dug into his luggage, selected a few essentials like bandages and adhesive tape and a left shoe, and slipped them into a shoulder bag.

The pilot met them at the gate. Teddy got out and leaned against the cab.

"You need a ride to the hangar?" the pilot said.

"No, I need you to take these bags and put them on my plane. I need to have the plane ready to go on a moment's notice."

"When?"

"This afternoon or tonight."

"I go home at seven."

"Not tonight you don't." Teddy slipped the pilot two hundred dollars. "You stay here so you can pick up more of these."

The pilot smiled. "Yes, I do."

"Where to now?" the cabbie said as they drove off.

"You know the Golden Grill?"

"Sure."

"We're going somewhere near it."

"Near it?"

"Just drive by. I'll tell you where to stop."

They drove back to the main strip. Teddy kept his head down passing the New Desert Inn and Casino. It was silly to think anyone might see him, but just that sort of long shot had ruined more than one agent's mission when he was with the CIA.

"Here we are," the cabbie said. "It's up ahead on the left."

"Go on by and make a U-turn at the next corner, or go around the block—whatever you need to do to get back to that corner going the other way."

The cabbie checked traffic and had no problem pulling a U-turn.

"Okay," Teddy said. "Drive down the street and stop two driveways down from the restaurant."

Two driveways down from the Golden Grill was an all-night diner.

"Pull in there."

The driver pulled in the driveway and parked.

"Perfect," Teddy said. "You're going to be here for a while. You got something to read?"

"I got a paperback thriller."

"Well, don't believe a word of it. That type of stuff never happens. I probably won't be back until after six, but don't count on it. Go in, get yourself a sandwich to go, and eat it in the car. That way you're a customer and they can't bitch about you taking up the spot. If you need something else, get it, but get it to go and get it fast. I may have to leave in a hurry."

"But probably not till after six?"

"That's how it is." Teddy handed him two more hundreds. "We good?"

"We're good."

Teddy pulled up his pant leg and took off his cast.

The cabbie's mouth fell open.

"And you're not reporting this," Teddy said, and slapped another two hundred bucks in his hand.

Teddy took a pair of surgical gloves out of the bag and slipped them on. Out of sight of the driver, he took his gun out of his shoulder holster and replaced it with the gun that killed Ace Vargas, checking to be sure it was fully loaded.

When he was all set, he pulled the shoe out of the bag and slipped it on his bare foot. He left the cast, the crutches, and the bag of medical supplies on the floor of the backseat, got out, and hobbled behind the diner.

97

The stairs up from the basement of the Golden Grill had metal cellar doors that slanted from the ground a few feet up the back wall of the restaurant. They were locked, of course, but Teddy wasn't going in. Instead, he scrambled up the incline. He pulled himself up and peered through the window.

It was just as he figured when he scouted it out. He had a clear view of the private dining room. He could see every seat at the table.

And he couldn't be seen himself. The back of the Golden Grill was fenced off from its neighbors. It was a pain in the ass to get through, but Teddy had solved tougher problems, broken leg or not. It took him fewer than five minutes to break the bottom off enough slats to squirm through.

It was almost harder pulling himself up the slanted cellar door. He hadn't climbed with only one leg before. It was doable, but it wasn't fun. He got in position and checked his watch.

He was early—it was only a quarter to five—but he wouldn't be going down and up again. He was there for the duration.

Sammy's goons appeared at five. There were four of them, most likely mobsters from Jersey—tough, dangerous, and none too bright. It didn't matter, as long as they were packing heat. They scouted out the room, checked the chairs and the sideboards. Teddy couldn't imagine what they were looking for, but they did it.

One of them looked out the window. Teddy had to cling to the sill with his fingertips, his body hanging off the side of the cellar door.

He didn't open the window. Had the goon been in his employ, Teddy would have fired him for such negligence. In this case, he blessed him for it instead.

Sammy Candelosi showed up at a quarter to six, accompanied by his henchman, Slythe. Teddy recognized him immediately as the substitute prop man. To a pro like Teddy, the rudimentary disguise of tucking his hair into a baseball cap was incredibly feeble.

Sammy spoke to his men, assigning seats at the table. Teddy suppressed a laugh. He couldn't help thinking of a hostess arranging place cards at a dinner party.

It wasn't complicated. Sammy would be seated at the head of the table with Slythe seated to his right, and Mason and Gerard to his left. The other goons would fill in the sides.

Ironing that out took longer than it should have. By the time they were finished, it was almost six. The stage was set, the curtain was about to go up.

It was time for Mason and Gerard's entrance.

The phone rang in Mason and Gerard's suite. Mason picked it up. "Yes?"

"Your limousine is downstairs."

Mason hung up. "Our limo's here."

"Excellent," Gerard said. He checked the gun in his shoulder holster.

Mason sighed. "I don't like you wearing a gun."

"It'll be fine," Gerard said, and pushed him toward the door.

The concierge guided them out front where a stretch limo was waiting. The driver stood holding the door.

"Good evening, gentlemen. I'll be taking you to the Golden Grill. It's a five-minute ride, but there is champagne and caviar if you would like."

The limo let them out right in front of the Golden Grill. The maître d' met them at the door. "Do you have a reservation?"

"Kimble and Cardigan. We're dining with Mr. Candelosi."

"Ah, yes, you're in the private dining room. Right this way, please."

The maître d' took them himself, part of the VIP treatment.

They went in and immediately found their way blocked by two large goons. Sammy Candelosi stood behind them.

"Gentlemen. Do come in. I hope you don't mind the imposition, but my boys need to pat you down."

Mason felt a cold chill in the pit of his stomach. This was exactly what he'd dreaded. The goons would find Gerard's gun and take it away from him and shoot him.

Gerard's reaction was just the opposite. He took a step back from the two goons and said calmly, "Then this meeting is over. My friend doesn't have a gun, but I do, and so do all your men. If you expect me to sit unarmed in a room where everyone else has a weapon, I cannot believe you'd make a deal with that kind of schmuck. I'll show you my gun. It's in a shoulder holster." He flipped his jacket open and displayed the weapon. "You're not going to shoot me at the dinner table, and I'm not about to shoot you. So do you want to have dinner, or should we go?"

Sammy Candelosi chuckled. He wished Gerard worked for him. He was sorry he had to kill him. "Fine, keep your gun. I can't wait to find out what this is all about."

Mason had recovered his poise. "You're the one who wanted the meeting."

A waiter appeared and took their drink orders. When he left there was an awkward silence, each group expecting the other to initiate the business conversation. Since there was no proposal to discuss, nothing happened.

Sammy was amused by the situation. He wondered when the boys planned to make their move. He prolonged the suspense by passing out cigars.

The waiter came back with their drinks. He served everyone and went out.

Sammy raised his drink. "Cheers," he said.

His eyes twinkled.

99

Teddy was pleased to see everyone had guns, and that Sammy had let Gerard keep his. He wondered what would have happened if he had tried to take it away. Gerard wouldn't have stood for it.

Mason Kimble was another story. He looked freaked out by the situation, which was actually perceptive on his part. Sammy Candelosi was not acting like a man who was taking a meeting, no matter how much he smiled and offered drinks. The conversation was stilted at best. Neither party had a business deal to discuss. Of course, Sammy knew there *was* no business deal, but Mason Kimble didn't, and per Teddy's instructions he was waiting for Sammy to bring it up.

The silence was excruciating.

Teddy figured it was time to get the party started. He took out the Ace Vargas gun, aimed it through the windowpane, and shot Slythe right between the eyes.

Pandemonium erupted.

As Slythe slumped to the table, everyone went for their

guns. Gerard actually got off a shot before a hail of bullets cut him down. His gun spun away from him across the room.

Sammy Candelosi, late on the draw, pumped a round into Gerard as he fell. Mason's lifeless body had already hit the floor, but Sammy and his goons were still firing at the corpses.

Under cover of the noise of their gunfire, Teddy smashed the glass in the window and shot Sammy Candelosi in the heart.

When the gunfire stopped, one goon realized his boss was down, and his yell alerted the others. They beat a quick exit, leaving the room empty but for the bodies.

Teddy tossed the Ace Vargas gun onto the floor between Mason Kimble and Gerard Cardigan.

100

The taxi driver was all keyed up when Teddy got back.

"I heard gunshots."

"I heard them, too," Teddy said. "Is that what that was?"

"They came from over there."

"I doubt it. I was over there."

"It sounded like they were in the restaurant."

"Well, that's it, then," Teddy said. "I wasn't in the restaurant."

The wail of police sirens approached.

"I guess it was gunshots," Teddy said. "What do you say we take off? I'd hate to be questioned as a witness, especially when I didn't see anything."

"I didn't see anything, but I heard the shots."

"Big deal, everyone on the block heard the shots. Come on, I gotta go."

"Where?"

"Back to the airport."

The cabbie gave Teddy a look. Teddy slapped money in his hand. "Get me to the airport on time and there'll be more."

The cab pulled out of the driveway just as police cars were stopping two doors down.

Teddy called the pilot to meet him at the gate. He got out his medical supplies and taped the cast back on his leg. He finished up just as they got there. Teddy slapped five hundred dollars into the cabbie's hand.

"That's for a job well done. You'll recall we toured the casinos. I didn't stay that long at any of them, but it took all day. And I was a lousy fare, just a cranky pain in the ass."

"The worst," the cabbie said with a grin.

Teddy took his crutches and his shoulder bag and got out. The pilot drove him to the hangar, where his plane was set to go. He tipped the pilot five hundred, got in his plane, and flew to Santa Monica.

Teddy set down on the runway and taxied up to Peter's hangar. The pilot came out to meet him.

"Good trip, Mr. Barnett?"

"Couldn't be better, but it's not quite over. Could you throw my bags in the car before you put the plane away?"

"Sure thing. Let me get it."

The pilot drove the car out of the hangar and tossed in the bags. Teddy thanked him, and sped into L.A.

He had one last thing to do.

101

The guests at Billy Barnett's housewarming party congregated on the terrace, attracted by the full-service bar, the climate-controlled swimming pool, and the charcoal grill serving burgers and barbecue ribs.

Teddy was holding forth at a table by the pool. He wasn't conducting any tours of the house, just letting people browse as they pleased. The only room he locked up was the study—he figured the huge safe Mike Freeman had installed might cause comment—but the other rooms were fair game. They included a movie theater/screening room that could seat fifty, a billiard room with a full-size pool table, an indoor lap pool should the weather prove inclement, a wine cellar, a bowling lane, a putting green, a four-car garage, and a workshop.

It also featured an elevator, a luxury for a three-story house, but a godsend for a man recovering from a broken leg.

Teddy had just gotten back. He'd finally gone on Billy Barnett's well-advertised but never actually realized vacation, excellent cover for a man who needed rehab.

While there he had called Sergeant O'Reilly as CIA agent Jonathan Foster, to let him know the Ace Vargas gun was no longer of interest in the agency investigation, and learned the case was almost closed. It appeared that movie producers Gerard Cardigan and Mason Kimble were killed in Las Vegas, in a shoot-out that also left a mobster and a couple of his henchmen dead. The gun that killed the mobster, and one of his henchmen, proved to be the Vargas gun, and the police investigation had discovered a link between Kimble and Cardigan and the deceased detective.

Teddy was relieved to hear it. He was glad he wouldn't have to point out the connection.

Ben Bacchetti and Mike Freeman came walking up.

Teddy grinned. "Ben. Where the hell'd you find him?"

"He was hanging around outside looking lonely."

"I didn't get an invitation," Mike said, "but I thought I'd crash."

"You didn't get an invitation because you're in New York. It's a long commute for a housewarming."

"You guys catch up," Ben said. "I'm getting ribs."

"I was just asking Ben about the hostile takeover," Mike said. "I understand it's over."

"The guys behind it got involved with mobsters and wound up dead." Teddy shrugged. "I don't know who their heirs are, but I doubt if they want to run a motion picture studio. We'll probably just buy back their stock. Anyway, the board meeting's canceled, thank God. Those things are a waste of time."

"Glad to hear it. So, how's your new security system?"

"Well, no one's burned the house down yet."

"What's the verdict on your old house?"

"Arson by person or persons unknown. That's cop-speak for we haven't got a clue. The insurance company's taking it to mean they don't have enough evidence to indict the guilty homeowner."

"Will you fight them?"

"Herbie Fisher offered to do it pro bono. It's the type of thing he's good at."

"The money's as good as yours." Mike lowered his voice. "Did you hear? Nigel Hightower's resurfaced."

"Really?" Teddy said.

"Yes. It's a load off my mind. Now the police will stop bugging me for information I don't have."

"Is he here in L.A.?"

"Chicago. He popped up on social media. According to Facebook, he has no intention of coming here."

Peter and Tessa showed up late. They'd been taping a radio interview to promote the movie.

Tessa came flying across the terrace. "Billy! How are you? Can I hug you, or are you still too sore?"

"It's nothing," Teddy said. "I slipped in the shower," he added, for the benefit of guests who didn't know he was Mark Weldon. "I'm fine now."

"Can you walk around?"

"Would you like a demonstration?" Teddy offered her his arm. "What can I show you?"

"Someplace quiet?"

"Would you like a drink?"

"I haven't talked to you in a month. Walk me out of earshot."

Teddy led Tessa into the library room. "See? Nothing quieter than a library."

Tessa grabbed his hands and looked into his eyes. "Is it over?"

"It's over. I have the last remaining physical copy, and the electronic file has mysteriously vanished from all of Mason Kimble's computers. I'll give you the DVD, and you can do whatever you want with it. But you're safe now. All the people who wanted to hurt you with it are dead."

"Thank God."

"Now that it's over, I strongly advise you to tell Ben about it. You'll feel better, and it's the right thing to do."

"I already did."

"Good girl."

Tessa smiled. Her eyes glistened. "I don't know how to thank you. If there's anything I can do for you, anything at all . . . "

Teddy considered. "Well, in the next movie we do together, could you stop upstaging me so damn much?"

Tessa laughed, and batted at him playfully.

AUTHOR'S NOTE

I am happy to hear from readers, but you should know that if you write to me in care of my publisher, three to six months will pass before I receive your letter, and when it finally arrives it will be one among many, and I will not be able to reply.

However, if you have access to the Internet, you may visit my website at www.stuartwoods.com, where there is a button for sending me e-mail. So far, I have been able to reply to all my e-mail, and I will continue to try to do so.

If you send me an e-mail and do not receive a reply, it is probably because you are among an alarming number of people who have entered their e-mail address incorrectly in their mail software. I have many of my replies returned as undeliverable.

Remember: e-mail, reply; snail mail, no reply.

When you e-mail, please do not send attachments, as I never open them. They can take twenty minutes to download, and they often contain viruses.

Please do not place me on your mailing lists for funny stories, prayers, political causes, charitable fund-raising, petitions, or sentimental claptrap. I get enough of that from people I already know. Generally speaking, when I get e-mail addressed to a large number of people, I immediately delete it without reading it.

Please do not send me your ideas for a book, as I have a policy of writing only what I myself invent. If you send me story ideas, I will immediately delete them without reading them. If you have a good idea for a book, write it yourself, but I will not be able to advise you on how to get it published. Buy a copy of *Writer's Market* at any bookstore; that will tell you how.

Anyone with a request concerning events or appearances may e-mail it to me or send it to: Publicity Department, Penguin Random House LLC, 375 Hudson Street, New York, NY 10014.

Those ambitious folk who wish to buy film, dramatic, or television rights to my books should contact Matthew Snyder, Creative Artists Agency, 9830 Wilshire Boulevard, Beverly Hills, CA 98212-1825.

Those who wish to make offers for rights of a literary nature should contact Anne Sibbald, Janklow & Nesbit, 445 Park Avenue, New York, NY 10022. (Note: This is not an invitation for you to send her your manuscript or to solicit her to be your agent.)

If you want to know if I will be signing books in your city, please visit my website, www.stuartwoods.com, where the tour schedule will be published a month or so in advance. If you wish me to do a book signing in your locality, ask your favorite bookseller to contact his Penguin representative or the Penguin publicity department with the request.

If you find typographical or editorial errors in my book and feel an irresistible urge to tell someone, please write to Sara Minnich at Penguin's address above. Do not e-mail your discoveries to me, as I will already have learned about them from others.

A list of my published works appears in the front of this book and on my website. All the novels are still in print in paperback and can be found at or ordered from any bookstore. If you wish to obtain hardcover copies of earlier novels or of the two nonfiction books, a good used-book store or one of the online bookstores can help you find them. Otherwise, you will have to go to a great many garage sales.